SALTY'S GOLD

Old Salty Parker rode into town every week with his little poke of gold dust and left it at the local bank. He was the last of the miners at Willard's Creek and the source of his gold was a mystery that many folk wanted to solve. Then a drifter was killed for asking too many questions and the bank was robbed after Salty let his tongue flap. But the trouble really began when the old miner was murdered and his granddaughter came to claim her inheritance.

1

The water in the creek was low and the old mine workings that lay beyond it were silted up by blown red sand. It settled on everything in the narrow valley that sheltered the creek as it ran down to the Gila River. The air was hot and dry, throwing a haze over the arid, tawny hills in the distance. There was not a cloud in the sky and the shadows thrown by a brilliant sun were hard and well defined.

The old man came out of his adobe hut and pulled the door shut behind him. His dog barked its protest at being left chained to the hitching post, but he gave it no more than a glance and shoved the Sharps rifle into the holster on the flank of his mule. There was a worn Navy Colt tucked into his belt and his old canvas pants were tucked into cracked Union Army half boots.

He mounted the mule and spat a generous portion of tobacco juice at the dog. The animal seemed contented with this little mark of affection and lay down placidly in the sun again, its tail wagging gently and its eyes alert.

The old rider turned his mount away from the creek towards the destination he aimed for every week whatever the weather. He was a small man, stoop-shouldered and in his seventies. His face was darkened by continual sun and his unkempt hair stuck out from the back of the old army hat he wore. His short beard was a straggly, uncombed mess of white whiskers that matched his ferocious eyebrows. His mouth was loose-lipped like an ageing moose but his washed-out blue eyes were alert enough to note everything that went on around him.

He rode slowly, not hurrying the big-boned mule that had served him uncomplainingly for the past ten years. The long valley held the heat of the day but it seemed to have no effect on him.

He passed the mine workings on the slopes without a glance. Only a few years before, men had laboured to bring out gold from every available source, but the veins had been exhausted and even the panning of the creek for dust had finally stopped. Salty Parker was the only miner left at Willard's Creek.

He came out of the valley onto the arid plain with its mesquite and low bushes and turned east to the little town of Willard that had been established in the heady days of the local gold rush. William Willard had made it rich in the narrow creek along the canyon bottom and hundreds had followed him to try their fortunes. Some had left rich men, but others had either never struck it lucky or had spent it all in the gambling dens and brothels that were set up for their convenience.

The gold rush was over; the town had quietened down, and only a few optimistic miners remained along the banks of the Gila and in the rugged red hills that housed more tarantulas than nuggets.

As Salty came round a scarp of multi-coloured rock, his eyes narrowed and he scanned the long ridge over to his left. A solitary Indian sat a pale horse and looked down at him. The old miner shaded his eyes to see better against the sun. The brave nursed a Springfield rifle in the crook of his left arm and raised his right ceremoniously towards the white man. Salty breathed a sigh of relief and returned the salute.

He rode steadily on, watching the distant Indian on the skyline and noting the others who joined him with a string of horses. They kept pace with Salty for a while and then gave a series of loud cries and vanished behind a ridge to gallop off to the north.

It was two hours later that he reached Willard. The town was one long main street with a series of shops and saloons on either side; some empty or neglected. The marshal's office was at the edge of town, opposite a dry goods

4

store that sold guns and ammunition. Salty steered his mount to the lawman's adobe jailhouse and dismounted wearily. He hitched the mule to the post and entered the little building.

'Mornin', Marshal,' he called out cheerfully. 'Got me some news for you.'

Marshal Tom Riley was seated at his desk, a cup of coffee in his hand and a game of patience laid out in front of him. 'Mornin', Salty,' he greeted the visitor. 'And what would that be then?'

'I seen me some Indians on the ridge just north of the creek. Six or seven of them with a herd of horses. They've been thievin' somewhere again.'

The marshal looked alert and put down the cup. He was a tall man in his late twenties with a fair skin reddened by the sun which had also bleached his short hair to a rich honey colour.

'Some of Delchay's boys?' he asked crisply.

The old man shrugged.

'Could be. Hard to tell when they all wear store clothes like Christian folk.

5

Armed with army rifles, they was, and a hell of a lot further south than they've been for years.'

The marshal drummed his fingers on the desk.

'General Crook is chasin' Delchay and Cochise all over the place, but the last I heard, he was up near Fort Apache and headin' towards Fort Barrett. Did they act hostile, Salty?'

The old man hesitated for a moment. 'Not to me,' he admitted. 'Just waved and scampered off. I got me no quarrel with the Apache.'

The marshal looked hard at him but did not push the matter.

'Well, thanks for the warnin',' he said. 'I'll tell the mayor and the storekeepers. We can't afford to have a night raid. Which way were they headin'?'

'North. Probably goin' to hole up in the hills. I reckon the horses they had will keep them pretty happy for now. But they're mighty close to town.'

The old man took his leave and, as he mounted his mule, the deputy marshal entered the office. He was a big man, older than his boss, with a round dark face and ragged black moustache that turned down at the corners.

'Old Salty makin' his usual visit?' he mused, as he crossed to the stove to pour himself some coffee.

The marshal held out his own cup for a refill.

'Yes. He spotted some Apaches by the creek. They had a string of extra horses with them and headed off up north. We'd better patrol all night, Mike, I don't like Indians so close to town.'

The deputy sat down and sipped his coffee.

'I often wonder about Salty Parker,' he said quietly. 'He lives up at the creek in that broken-down adobe hut with only an old coyote of a dog to protect him. Indians prowl around now and then, like they did a couple of years back, and then again today, but he always survives. I'm surprised he didn't lose his scalp years ago.'

The marshal grinned. 'I never liked to ask,' he admitted, 'but the folk around here tell me that his first wife was a Chiricahua squaw he bought from some homesteader. Treated her well he did and had two sons who went off to join Cochise a few years back. The Indians treat Salty like a tribal elder. I also got me a suspicion that he trades with them.'

'What's he got to trade?'

'Well, when I came here just after the war, there were a lot of old Springfields bein' disposed of by the Union Army. Salty had a few dollars at the time and he bought some. I think he traded them to his wife's people.'

'Couldn't you catch him at it?'

'No, he was too crafty. Besides, we had General Howard and that preacherman Smith spoutin' their nonsense at the time. The Indians were all God's children and could do no wrong. All the scalpin' and burnin' was all right with those fine gentlemen. They've learned their lesson, what with Skimmy promisin' somethin' new every five minutes, and Delchay and Cochise breakin' out all over the territory.'

He slammed down the coffee mug.

'And old Salty even recognized the guns them red devils was carryin',' he said angrily. 'He don't wear eyeglasses but he could tell me that they was totin' army rifles. The old rogue probably sold them to his Indian friends.'

'What exactly does he do in town every week?' the deputy asked.

'Goes to the bank. Has a few drinks in the Golden Nugget, gets in a few stores, and then goes home again, Pretty routine.'

'Why a visit to the bank?'

The marshal shook his head. 'I don't know, but he's never short of a few dollars. My guess is that he saved some of the money he made in the good old days and is drawin' on it now that the gold has run out. All the same, I'd like to be a blow-fly on the wall of that bank right now.'

If he had been a blow-fly on the wall

of the bank, the marshal would have seen old Salty at the counter. Carefully, he removed a small, soft leather bag from his waistcoat pocket and placed it in front of the clerk. The elderly teller brought a pair of brass scales and poured the contents on to one of the pans. It was a shiny pile of fine gold dust.

'Just five ounces as usual, Mr Parker,' he said obsequiously. 'You always have it measured out dead on the button.'

'I got my own scales, and I don't trust no money lenders,' Salty snapped.

The clerk looked affronted.

'We are bankers, Mr Parker . . . '

'Same thing. Just put that to my pile and I'll take ten dollars in dollar bills.'

'Certainly, sir.'

The clerk hesitated for a moment and then took the plunge. 'Wouldn't you like us to transfer all your gold to head office? There's over six hundred ounces now and that's quite a passel of money.'

Salty gave the man a long, hard stare.

'Look, fella, it's my gold and I'm kinda old-fashioned. I aim to get me one thousand ounces of the stuff, and then I'm goin' to the big city to retire. And I am goin' to live it up, friend. I am goin' to enjoy all the things I've missed while I've worked up to my ass in cold water and broken my back in some mine alongside tarantulas and Gila monsters. You gettin' the message?'

'Yes, Mr Parker. Of course.'

'Good. And I ain't just bein' ornery. The price of gold ain't goin' down and I reckon I'd do better by not changin' it to Yankee dollars any earlier than I need to.'

The clerk nodded reluctant defeat and entered the details in his ledger and in the little book that Salty presented.

When the miner had left, the clerk tapped on the door of the manager's office and was bidden enter. Pennington Wynn sat at a large roll-top desk in the far corner, his papers spread before him and his back to the big safe that stood open in all its green-painted splendour.

'Salty Parker has just been in, Mr Wynn. Usual deposit and withdrawal.'

The manager turned in his chair and took off the gold-rimmed glasses that normally perched on the end of his well-shaped nose. He was a short man but powerfully built and running to fat. His face was round and healthy, with a neatly trimmed moustache and long side-burns. His slight baldness was still being artfully hidden by pomaded wavy grey hair. His frock coat was well cut and his waistcoat edged with fashionable white piping.

'Never fails us,' he chuckled, taking out a large gold watch and checking the time. 'He must be the most punctual customer we have. Well, let's put it away with the rest of his treasure.'

While the clerk placed the pan of gold carefully on the desk, the manager crossed to the safe and brought out a white cotton bag that was heavy enough to need both hands. He dumped it on

12

the desk and started to undo the knotted string that held it shut.

'This really shouldn't be here,' he said ruefully, shaking his head.

'I told him that,' the clerk agreed self righteously. 'But he won't listen, Says he intends to build up a thousand ounces and then retire to the big city.'

'He'd be bored in a week. A thousand ounces? I'll get a rupture just picking up the damned bag and putting it on the desk. I sometimes wish the assay office hadn't closed down.'

'What I wonder,' the clerk said slyly, 'is where he gets it. Five ounces of good quality dust every week. He must be panning somewhere new.'

The manager shrugged. 'Either panning a new place or going over all the old areas and picking up a little bit here and there. If that's the case, he's certainly working the hard way.'

He waved the clerk back to his desk and began opening the heavy sack.

2

Old Salty did not remount his mule. He merely walked it along the street to the saloon which was still optimistically called the Golden Nugget. He tethered it there and went in for a drink before making a round of the stores to get his supplies for the week.

The saloon still housed three roulette tables that were seldom used and a couple of places for Faro. It was an ornately decorated building but the red and gold colours were fading and the brass foot-rails and spittoons needed polishing. Only one bartender was on duty and automatically he poured out Salty's usual measure of whiskey.

The old man paid with one of his newly acquired dollar bills and stood sipping it slowly as he looked around. The place was nearly empty and only one other man stood at the bar drinking a beer. He looked across at Salty and seemed about to say something. He was a tall man, thin and slightly stooped, well into his fifties and poorly dressed in serge pants and an old wool shirt. He was unshaven and his hair was grey and lank. He glanced at Salty again, hesitated a little, and then moved closer.

'I seen you at Willard's Creek,' he said quietly. 'Done seen what you do up there.'

Salty put down the whiskey and his right hand reached to his belt.

'So?' he murmured without inflexion.

'I had a claim up by the creek,' the other man said.

'A lotta folk have claims there, and they done give up on them,' Salty reminded him bluntly.

'You ain't given up.'

'No, I got my own ways of workin'.'

The man took a sip from his beer.

'I noticed,' he said. 'I watched you there.'

Salty's pale eyes were wary. The

15

stranger carried no gun but he wore a large Bowie knife in a soft leather scabbard.

'I ain't jumped no claims,' Salty said in a conciliatory manner. 'I just work the creek with a pan.'

'And you reckon to find dust?'

'I make out.'

'I tried panning. Never found nothin'. It was all worked out years ago.'

'What about your claim?'

'That was in the rocks up at the north end of the creek. I got me a couple of thousand dollars out of it a few years back . . . but it's all gone now; the lode petered out. You know how it is.'

'Yeah. The good days are over.'

The man moved nearer.

'I'd like to move on. Get me into California,' he said. 'Get to some place where there's still a hope of striking it rich.'

'Why don't you?'

The man shrugged hopelessly.

'I'd need grub-stakin',' he said.

'I don't think you've got much chance of that in this town,' Salty said unhelpfully.

'Oh, I don't know. There might be a fella who wouldn't want it spread around how he gets his gold.'

There was a long silence while both men sipped their drinks with the delicacy of two elderly ladies taking coffee at a prayer meeting. It was Salty who broke the silence.

'And you figure on me grub-stakin' you?' he asked softly.

'Why not?'

The old miner grinned wolfishly. 'It'd be easier to kill you,' he said.

The other man nodded agreement.

'You might do that, friend, but I can pull this knife and stick it in your gut as fast as you can pull that gun. And we're nice and close right now, ain't we?'

'You've got a point. So how do you think I get my gold?'

The man grinned slyly. 'I seen you with the Apache. You're tradin' with 'em. Sure as damn it.'

'Is that a fact, now?' Salty chuckled with relief. 'Then why don't you go and tell that to the marshal? He's just down the street.'

'I ain't a troublemaker. I just need me a stake and I'll be away from here.'

Salty thought about it.

'And how much would it cost me?' he asked.

The man licked his lips. 'I ain't greedy. Fifty dollars?' he suggested tentatively.

'Well, you certainly ain't greedy, I'll say that for you.'

Salty took the man by the arm and led him gently but firmly to the door of the saloon. He pointed at a building in the distance.

'That's the marshal's office,' he said. 'Take your story to him and see if he'll stake you.'

'You're bluffin'.'

'Try me.'

Salty left him and went back to the bar. He ordered another whiskey and leaned on the counter, ignoring the man who stood uncertainly in the doorway. Finally he came back to join the old miner.

'All right, maybe I was a bit out of line,' he said humbly, 'but I need a stake bad, and you're a miner, like me. You know how it is. Just fifty dollars.'

Salty put his glass on the counter.

'That's more like it,' he said. 'I'll grub-stake any miner down on his luck, but I don't take kindly to bein' pushed. I have a habit of pushin' back. Now, I got some chores to do around town but I'll go see the bank this afternoon. We'll meet somewhere tonight. Does that suit you?'

'Thanks.' The man's face lit up. 'Let's meet here.'

'Don't you trust me in a lonely place?'

They both grinned mirthlessly, gauging each other.

'I don't trust nobody,' the man said. 'But I ain't the talkative type. You've nothin' to worry about.'

19

'I'm not worryin',' Salty assured him. 'See me here at ten o'clock tonight. And don't be late 'cos I want to get home while the moon's still high.'

★　★　★

It got no cooler when the sun went down, and the air hung heavy over Willard, with not a breath of wind to stir the red dust in the main street. Salty had done all his buying and strapped the goods on his mount in good military style. The dry goods merchant helped him distribute the load and tie it on with a basic diamond hitch. The animal submitted meekly. The load was less than Salty's weight and the old man would have to walk at the side of his mule. He took the animal across to the Golden Nugget just before ten o'clock and hitched it to the rail alongside the few horses that were there.

The thin miner was already at the bar, drinking a beer and watching four elderly men playing poker. He brightened up when Salty entered and even ordered him a whiskey. The old man took it and nodded his thanks.

'I got your stake,' he said flatly. 'Five bills of ten dollars apiece. You got a horse?'

'A mule. Same as you. Why?'

''Cos when you leave here, you go straight to wherever it's hitched and you get yourself outa town. If I see your face again, I'll start shootin' before gettin' in range of that knife.'

He took the folded notes out of his pocket and handed them across. The man took them eagerly and counted each one.

'I'll be long gone before you leave this bar,' he assured the old man.

Salty nodded silently and watched his companion swallow the last of his beer and head for the door.

It was about ten minutes later that the shot rang out.

3

There was a sudden silence in the saloon and everybody stopped what they were doing. Salty put down his drink and headed for the door. Several other people followed and they all stood on the wooden sidewalk, looking up and down the badly lit street. The marshal came running from the jailhouse with a shotgun in his hand. He was closely followed by the lumbering deputy.

'Where was it?' the lawman asked.

They all looked at each other, and a man who had been in the street when the shot was fired, pointed down towards the livery stable.

'Somewhere back there,' he shouted.

The marshal and his deputy hurried down the street followed by the gathering crowd.

'Do you think it's them Indians?' the

22

deputy gasped as he ran.

'I doubt it,' Marshal Riley replied tersely. 'There'd have been more than one shot.'

He stopped at the front of the livery stable and noted the lights going on in the bedroom above the feed store. A head poked out of the window and shouted down.

'Somewhere behind my corral, Marshal,' the man yelled. 'I can see a body from the back window.'

A few torches and a couple of oil lanterns were on the scene by now as people came out of their houses. The marshal hurried round the corner, shotgun at the ready, the flickering lights throwing uncertain shadows over the scene.

Ahead of him was the corral of the livery stable. Half-a-dozen horses were milling around nervously, whinnying their distress. A few yards in front of them, a dark figure lay on the red dust, face down and with arms outstretched. The marshal turned the man over and everyone saw the massive bloodstain on the ground.

'Anybody know him?' Tom Riley asked.

'He was in the saloon earlier,' somebody said uncertainly.

'That's right,' Salty butted in. 'I was talkin' to him. He left a few minutes ago.'

'Anybody know his name?' the marshal asked.

There was a general shaking of heads. The doctor had arrived now and he made a quick examination.

'Not a job for me,' he said cheerfully. 'I figure it's another customer for Joe Sykes.'

Joe Sykes was the mortician and he was already hurrying along the street in happy anticipation of business.

'Can you take a look through his pockets, Doc?' the marshal asked.

'Afraid of getting blood on your hands, son?' the medical man suggested slyly.

'No, but I reckon there's no call for

24

both of us to get mussed up. I suppose you can tell us how he died?'

The doctor started searching the body.

'He died of a single gunshot wound,' he said formally. 'Right through the centre of the chest at very close range. There's powder burns on his shirt and, if it matters, the bullet is still in the body.'

He displayed what he had found on the corpse. A couple of silver dollars, some small change, a wad of chewing tobacco, and a folded sheet of paper. The marshal took the document and motioned one of the lantern holders to come nearer.

'It's a mine registration,' he said as he read it. 'Five years old and made out in the name of Edward Forbes. Well, at least we have a name for him.'

The body was finally carried away and the crowd gradually dispersed. After a fruitless search around the town, the marshal and his deputy returned to the jailhouse and were followed by Salty Parker. He entered with them and waited silently until the lawman locked up the few items found on the corpse.

'As I mentioned back there, marshal,' he said quietly, 'I spoke to this Forbes fella in the saloon. He told me that he was down on his luck and wanted to try California. So I grub-staked him.'

The marshal looked at the old man in surprise.

'How much?' he asked.

'Fifty dollars. In ten-dollar bills.'

The marshal whistled. 'So we know what he was killed for,' he said grimly.

'I reckon so.'

'Did anyone follow him out of the saloon?'

Salty shrugged. 'I wasn't payin' no heed,' he admitted. 'I got to watchin' the poker game.'

'Well, thanks for tellin' me, Salty. At least we know why he was bush-whacked. I was thinkin' of Indians for a moment, but they'd have shot wild and whooped it up. Now we know different. But who the hell would do it?'

The deputy was heating coffee on the stove.

'We got no strangers in town that I know of,' he said. 'All the folk in the saloon were locals. Nobody seems to have heard a horse gallopin' away either.'

'Somebody must have seen me give him the money,' Salty said thoughtfully. 'Maybe they think I've got more on me. I reckon I'll take my burro down to the livery stable and put up in their barn for the night. I don't fancy travellin' in the dark after this.'

'I think you're wise, Salty,' the marshal said. 'Mike and I are goin' to be on call all night anyhow after that Indian sightin'.'

'I don't reckon they'll trouble us none,' Salty said, 'but you can never tell what they'll do if they're full of corn liquor or just feelin' ornery.'

The old man bade them a goodnight and took his laden mule down to the livery stable where the owner was still awake after all the disturbance.

⋆　⋆　⋆

The marshal escorted Salty home the next day. He wanted to check that the Apaches were out of the area and had already sent a telegraph message to several of the forts where General Crook might be located. He left the old man at his broken-down shack and went on along the creek and up to the ridge where the Indians had been sighted. There were signs of them; unshod horses and some with iron shoes that had probably been stolen from a ranch. Their tracks headed north and he followed as far as was practicable to make sure that they did not turn back towards the town.

Tom Riley was a conscientious man. He took his responsibilities very seriously and was annoyed that a killing had taken place in his town without there being the slightest sign of knowing who had done it. He turned back eventually, scanning the distant hills and sweating on the old McClellan saddle that he used as a matter of habit. He saw a figure in the distance, heading east on a mule, and realized that it was Salty Parker. He wondered what the old man was doing now as he watched him disappear over the horizon, heading for the junction of the Santa Cruz river and Fort Barrett.

The job of marshal was a pretty routine one in Willard. Without the miners it had become a dull town and, except for an occasional Indian scare or some gunfight between otherwise law-abiding folk, the peace officers had a quiet life. There were times when the marshal wished it could be different. He still missed something of the excitement of the war when he had served for the last two years in the army of the Confederacy. He had no particular political convictions but he was a southerner and did what all the other locals did. He rode back to town in a thoughtful mood.

*   *   *

The next few weeks passed peacefully in Willard. The sun blistered the town as usual, Salty Parker paid a visit each week, and the stagecoach passed through more or less on time but brought no new faces and little of interest from the rest of the world. News came from Fort McDowell that Delchay and a dozen braves had attacked a farm on the Gila River and made off with some horses after slaughtering the family there. They were now somewhere north of the fort and had outrun a detachment of troops sent out from Fort Whipple.

The news meant that Willard was safe for the foreseeable future, and everyone breathed a sigh of relief.

It was on a Monday morning that things began to happen in the town. Marshal Riley slept in the jailhouse and was late rising that day. He had been up part of the night investigating a family row out at the Miller farm. The old man was drunk as usual and was beating up his wife while the children screamed and the eldest one ran into town to call on the lawman to do something about it. He had ridden over and floored the bullying homesteader with a blow on the jaw that had silenced him for the rest of the weekend. By the time he got back to town, the marshal was tired and angry, and consequently slept late.

His deputy was in the office when he awoke, explaining to an agitated townswoman that a straying dog rooting up her garden was not a job for the law.

The marshal sat down at his desk and accepted the cup of coffee that Mike Pearce placed before him.

'I reckon that's about as excitin' as it's goin' to get,' he said sleepily. 'One stray dog and a drunken old farmer who beats up on his family. I figure the

31

rest of the week is goin' to seem rather dull after a start like that.'

The deputy was looking out of the window at the man who was tethering his horse at the jailhouse hitching post.

'Don't talk too soon, Tom,' he said. 'We've got ourselves another customer.'

The man who entered was broad and dark, with a slightly Mexican appearance that was enhanced by a large black moustache. He wore an old Confederate jacket and by the time he was through the door, he held a Colt Army model in each hand. The hammers were drawn back and the pistols pointed steadily at the two lawmen.

'I don't want no one to be a hero,' he said tautly. 'Just get yourselves into one of them cells, and then throw the key out to me.'

The marshal rose from his chair and his hand went automatically to his belt. Then he realized that he had not yet put on his gun, and neither had his deputy. Even had they been armed, the stranger was at an advantage. Tom Riley pulled a wry face and opened the desk drawer for the cell keys. The Colt waved a warning at him in case he had thoughts of taking out more than the keys.

He opened one of the cell doors and walked slowly inside. Mike Pearce followed reluctantly, his belligerent expression making it quite clear that he would have liked to take on the stranger at the least opportunity. Tom Riley locked the door and flung the bunch of keys across the office to land on the top of his desk. They slid across the worn leather top and ended up on the floor near the feet of the man holding the guns. The stranger put one of his pistols on half-cock, tucked it into his belt, and picked up the keys. He stuck them into the pocket of his pants and then tried the door of the cell with his free hand.

'That was good thinkin', fellas,' he said, a little more cheerfully. 'Let's keep it that way 'cos I don't figure on killin' nobody unless I have to. Ain't in my nature to be cruel to dumb lawmen.'

'So what happens now?' the marshal asked, with all the dignity he could muster.

'We wait.'

'For what?'

'For me to go. Now, just set yourselves down on them bunks and keep quiet. The first one to make a noise gets dead. So let's all do it the easy way and not get excited.'

He looked around the office, took a glance out of the window, and finally holstered the other gun and poured himself a cup of coffee. It smelled good and the marshal looked longingly at his own cup still steaming on the desk.

'Can I have my coffee from off the desk there?' he asked.

The man grinned.

'I ain't stupid enough to hand anything through the bars, Marshal. You'll just have to wait awhile. But don't worry. we ain't aimin' to stick around your town all day.'

He crossed to the window again and

stood looking out at the street scene. Mike Pearce had both large hands on the bars as though he would snap them like some infuriated Titan. The marshal shook his head in a gesture of patience. He did not want the stranger to see how much they were being humiliated. Instead, he concentrated on memorizing the man's features for use on a Wanted poster.

It was some ten minutes later that their captor moved from his position. He took one of the guns from its ex-army holster and waved it in their direction.

'I'm leavin' now,' he said, 'and you can holler all you want. By the time your friends get you out of there, we'll be long gone.'

He opened the door and stepped out onto the broadwalk. They caught a glimpse of several horses milling around outside the jailhouse and then the door was slammed shut and they were alone. Receding hootbeats echoed along the street.

'They've robbed the bank,' Tom Riley said grimly.

'You think so?' Mike seemed doubtful. 'We didn't hear any shootin'.'

The marshal grimaced. 'They didn't do any shootin' here,' he said, 'but they sure as hell dealt with us. It was as smooth as silk, Mike. He took us like a couple of hicks while the rest of them were doin' something similar down the street. We'd better start yellin' out the back window. We'll look mighty foolish but we gotta do it. Break that glass.'

It was fully three-quarters of an hour before anyone heard them and came to help, and it was not because of their shouting but because a customer had entered the bank and found all the staff and a woman customer bound and gagged in the manager's office. He had hurriedly released them and then rushed to the marshal's office only to make a second discovery. He then had to go for the blacksmith and it was another humiliating half an hour before the lawmen were released with the aid of a hammer and chisel. Two very embarrassed peace officers finally made their way along the street to the bank. A large crowd had gathered by then and they had to push their way through it.

There were a few jeers and witty remarks as the red-faced marshal went through to where the lady customer was having hysterics and Mr Wynn and his staff of two were still rubbing their wrists to restore the circulation.

'Well, it took you long enough,' the manager snapped. 'We could all have been killed . . . !'

'Now, hold it, Mr Wynn,' the marshal held up a restraining hand. 'We've all had our troubles this morning so you'd better just tell me what happened.'

'Shouldn't you be after them?'

'They've had over an hour's start so they're ten to fifteen miles away by now in any direction. We've got to get a posse together and then hire some Indian trackers to find out what route they took. I can't get the trackers till mornin', so there's no point in goin' off half-cock. Just tell me what happened here, then I'll go down to the telegraph office and notify all the lawmen in the territory. If I send a message to the nearest forts, the army will pass it along, and everyone will be lookin' for them.'

The manager thought about it for a moment.

'Sounds reasonable,' he conceded. 'I suppose you know your own business. Two men came in just after we opened. I was in the office and the next thing I knew, Bill, Eddy and Mrs Morgan came through the door with two men covering them with shotguns. There was absolutely nothing we could do. They just emptied the safe and the cash drawers, took our watches and Mrs Morgan's gold brooch. Then they tied us up and gagged us.'

'How much is missing?'

'Precisely three thousand two hundred and twenty-three dollars in notes. One hundred and eleven dollars in coins. The coins are in paper bags.'

The manager took a deep breath as if the next part of the story was really going to hurt him.

'And they took Salty Parker's gold dust,' he said in a small voice.

'And how much would that be worth?'

The manager took another deep breath.

'At sixteen dollars an ounce, it comes to ten thousand, two hundred and forty dollars, give or take a few cents,' he said mournfully.

Mike Pearce let out a loud whistle.

'He must be the richest man in the territory,' he said admiringly.

'Not any more,' the marshal muttered.

'The politicos are the richest men in the territory,' Mr Wynn said to keep the record straight. 'However, Salty's money is quite safe. The bank takes full responsibility even if we did advise against leaving so much gold on deposit.'

'This gold . . . ' the marshal ventured, . . . 'it must weigh quite a bit?'

'About forty pounds. It's in a white cotton bag with the bank's name stencilled on it in blue letters. Salty is going to be very unhappy about it though. I'm told that he was aiming at a thousand ounces. I don't think dollar bills will mean quite as much to him. However, beggars can't be choosers.'

'I reckon not,' said the marshal. 'He's lucky, all the same.'

'I doubt if he'll be grateful.'

The marshal looked at his deputy and told him to take the clerks outside and get some descriptions of the hold-up men from them. Then he turned his attention to the manager again.

'Tell me, Mr Wynn,' he said, 'how in hell's name did Salty get six hundred-odd ounces of gold dust together? That's what we're talkin' about, ain't it? Forty pounds weighs something like that.'

'Your arithmetic is very good, Marshal. Six hundred and forty ounces, to be precise.'

'No other panner has produced a fraction of that in the past five years.'

The manager sat down at his desk and opened one of the many drawers. He took out a bottle of branded whiskey and a couple of glasses. The marshal accepted a drink and watched Mr Wynn swallow his own eagerly.

'I needed that,' the manager said, as he poured himself another. 'This has been the most frightening moment of my life. Now, about Salty. He always panned a few ounces when things were good up at the creek. Nothing very big but he made a living. Of course, it all went to the assay office in those days and he had a normal savings account with us. Still has, in fact. But about two years ago he came in with one hundred and twenty ounces of good quality river dust. Wouldn't have it changed into cash, but just wanted us to hold it for him, apparently until he reached this

41

thousand-ounce target. Every week since then, he's brought five ounces of gold dust to add to his stock. Regular as clockwork he's been. He must be re-panning the creek somewhere along the line, but he's too cagey to tell anybody where he's working.'

The marshal shook his head doubtfully.

'I don't know about that,' he said slowly. 'From all I hear tell, Salty's a bit of an old rogue. I wonder if the Confederacy or the Union lost any gold shipments in this area during the war. Did you ever hear tell of anything like that happening?'

The manager shook his head.

'I've been in Willard since '63,' he said, 'and I've never heard tell of such a thing. Are you suggesting that Salty didn't pan for it?'

'Well, I have my doubts. Have there been any other robberies where dust has been stolen?'

'Not that I recall, and a quantity like that would be pretty hard to overlook.'

The marshal finished his drink and got up to go.

'Well, I'll get me down to the telegraph office now and send out the messages. Then I'll ride over to Mackin's farm and hire his Apache guides. They're pretty old but he keeps them on his payroll and they know their business. They used to hunt down runaway slaves in the old days. Mackin made himself quite a bundle of dollars out of that trade. I reckon he'd still shoot any Yankee who was fool enough to ride on his land. We'll need a posse of six or seven men, and I'll let Mike handle that while I'm at Mackin's place. I think we have a good chance of recoverin' everything.'

The marshal stopped in the doorway.

'Do you happen to know Salty's real name, Mr Wynn?' he asked.

The manager looked puzzled for a moment. 'Well, now . . . ' he began, 'I'd have to check our ledger . . . '

'It's Nathaniel,' the marshal told him. 'Nathaniel Thomas Parker. He was called Salty by people who knew what he did for a livin', and I guess the name stuck.'

'And what . . . what was that living, Marshal?'

'He sold fake gold mines.'

4

The elderly Apache Indians arrived in town the next day and the marshal and his deputy managed to get a posse of men to join them in the hunt for the bank robbers. They set out just after noon with the scouts circling around until they found a trail heading south. This confirmed what one of the townsfolk had indicated when he saw three horsemen travelling towards the high southern ridges as he headed home from a trip to Fort Barrett. The times fitted, and the posse rode with confidence that they were on the right trail. Descriptions of the men had been circulated by telegraph and army patrols were already quartering the area in the hope of crossing the tracks.

The posse rode all day, following a definite trail of hoof prints and broken grass tufts which told the Indian guides how long it had been since someone passed that way. The heat was relentless and reflected from the rocks as they passed through narrow gorges and over barren outcrops.

There was not much doubt that the hold-up men were heading for Mexico and, once across the border, would be much harder to capture. The marshal's authority would cease and the Mexican Army, no lovers of the Americans, would be eager to repel a posse. Marshal Riley pushed on his men ruthlessly, ignoring the heat and only concerned with his own humiliation at the hands of the robbers.

Back in Willard, things were dropping back into the normal routine. The local people had got over the excitement and were now more interested in the story about the local preacher man and his consumption of whiskey.

Salty Parker rode into town a couple of days after the hold-up. It was his usual weekly visit and he was still unaware of the loss of his gold. He was taken into the manager's office when he reached the bank, and spent a long time there in conversation with Mr Wynn. When he came out again, the clerks noticed his flushed face and the distinct smell of the manager's good quality drinking liquor. Mr Wynn himself saw Salty to the door, his arm on his shoulder, and sympathy in his every hushed word. Salty left the bank in a daze.

'He didn't leave any gold dust today,' the elderly clerk ventured, as he watched the miner collect his mule and walk it down the street.

'I think he's lost confidence in us,' the manager said sourly.

'And he didn't withdraw his usual ten dollars for living expenses.'

The manager shrugged. 'I assume he can manage, and I suppose he still has the five ounces of gold he would normally have left here. I must confess that I'm still a little too shaken to worry about Salty Parker. After all, he still has the value of the gold when head office send us the money in dollar bills.'

'Is he going to withdraw it all?'

'Every last cent of it, so he says. And he'll probably close his savings account as well. There's a few hundred dollars in that, as I recall. He wasn't very pleasant about it, so I rather think I'll be glad to see the back of the old goat.'

'He didn't take the news well then, Mr Wynn?'

'He was furious. I explained that he wouldn't be the loser, but that wouldn't do at all. I think he just wanted to be the owner of a thousand ounces of gold dust. He wanted to actually hold it; to know that it was a reality. I suppose I should feel sorry for him because I can see his point of view.'

Salty went to the dry goods store to get some flour and bacon, but found it impossible to change his dust for cash money. He tried at one or two of the other stores, but it was the same story. None of them had scales that would measure an ounce or two of gold, and none of them were really prepared to deprive themselves of ready cash for a precious metal that could only be changed at the bank. They all gave him credit though, and he was able to load up his mule as usual.

It was early evening before he went along to the Golden Nugget for a drink. That was the one place he could be sure of getting cash for some of his dust. He had left home relying on the usual ten dollars and the upset at the bank had simply driven it from his mind until he got to the stores. The effect of Mr Wynn's whiskey was now wearing off and he fancied a drop of the rougher stuff he was used to.

The Golden Nugget was quite busy and several drinkers were lined up at the bar. The oil lamps had been lit and there was a friendly atmosphere in the place. The bartender poured out Salty's drink and he stood savouring it after paying with the few coins he had in his pocket.

'Jess,' he said quietly, 'I got me some dust I'd like to change into dollar bills.'

The bartender nodded and went to fetch the scales. The other drinkers looked on with mute curiosity.

'How much, Salty?' he asked.

The old man drew the little leather bag from his waistcoat pocket.

'I reckon a couple of ounces will do for now,' he said, as he began to untie the string.

'Ten dollars to the ounce.'

'Ten dollars! My God! That's daylight robbery!'

Everybody in the saloon heard the miner's agonized protests.

The bartender shrugged with total indifference.

'Boss's orders,' he said calmly. 'He's gotta make a profit and ten dollars is top price for fine dust or nuggets. It's take it or leave it.'

'I can get me fifteen dollars from the bank, and they're cheatin' at that price. Come on, Jess, give me fourteen dollars and I'll call you a Christian man.'

'Sorry, Salty. Ten's the limit.'

The old miner swore under his

breath and put the little chamois bag back into his pocket.

'Never mind then,' he snarled. 'Just give me another whiskey and I'll be on my way.'

Salty rolled out of the saloon an hour later, unhitched his mule and headed for home. The moon was high and the stars brilliant, but the cursing old man heeded nothing except his grudge against the Golden Nugget.

★   ★   ★

Marshal Riley's posse rounded the edge of a long yellow-coloured scarp and saw the ruined farm ahead of them. The Indian scouts had found it the night before and the lawmen had ridden through the darkness to get to the place and into position by break of day. It was a bleak area, with just enough grazing for a few cattle, fed by a stream that sometimes ran dry in the summer heat. Indians had raided it a few years back and killed the family that had lived there. Nobody had bothered to occupy it since and it lay in a semi-ruined state.

The farm buildings were of crude white adobe, blackened by fire and with parts of the wall missing. The house itself was roofless, its windows without glass and only a gap in the wall for a door. Most of the fencing was down and a low scrub had grown all round the place. There were three horses in one of the corrals. They were tethered by their bridles, chomping at a pile of grass that had been placed there for them.

Smoke came from the chimney of the battered house.

The Indian guides stood impassively as the marshal surveyed the scene. He gave them his thanks for their work but only got blank stares from men who were not involved in his problems.

'All right,' he said cheerfully, 'they seem to be the coyotes we're after. So let's not make a mess of things. The scouts can go in quietly and remove the horses. Then we'll surround the building, cover each window and the doorway; we'll have them trapped. They're obviously cookin' a meal so we'd better get movin' fast in case they decide to be on their way.'

He motioned to the two Indians and they nodded enigmatically and ran silently on moccasined feet towards the distant corral. Each carried an old Springfield rifle, but across their backs were the far more useful bows and arrows.

'And one more thing,' the marshal enjoined his posse, 'I want them alive if possible. So don't start shootin' till I've called on them to come out peaceful. Bank robbin' ain't a hangin' matter, more's the pity, so we gotta try and take them alive.'

'And what if they don't come out quietly?' Mike Pearce asked fiercely.

'Then we go in shootin'. We'll have no choice; it'll be their decision.'

Everybody eagerly agreed and they began to dismount and unholster their rifles. Marshal Riley made his way down the rock-strewn slope, making sure that they all kept low and disturbed as little scree as possible. The two Indians were already at the corral among the horses. Their hands were gently covering nervous muzzles as they untied the ropes and led the animals away.

Riley waved to the scouts to take the mounts clear away from the farm as he and the posse closed in and settled themselves behind the plentiful rocks that were within shooting range. The men lay down quietly, keeping an eye on the marshal or his deputy. Mike had three men covering one side and the rear of the little building. Tom Riley and the other men covered the front and the other side. They were close enough to hear voices from within the house and there was a strong smell of coffee and bacon.

The marshal stood up and shouted. 'You in there!' he bellowed. 'You're covered by a marshal's posse so drop your guns and come out peaceful.'

There was a long silence, and then a rifle barrel appeared slowly in the opening of one of the windows.

'And what marshal would that be?' a voice shouted back.

'Marshal Riley from Willard. If you're the fellas what robbed the bank there, we aim to take you in. If you ain't the folk we're huntin' for, we won't trouble you no further. So come on out and let's take a look at you.'

There was another long silence and some slight movement could be seen beyond the window spaces.

The marshal tried again. 'I don't want no killin'!' he yelled. 'Bank robbin' ain't a hangin' offence. You'll get a fair trial at Fort Barrett.'

'You gotta take us first, Marshal,' the voice jeered at him. 'We ain't aimin' to visit Fort Barrett. Not unless they gotta bank we could take a fancy to.'

The marshal turned to the man at his side and grinned.

'Well, we know they're the ones,' he

said in a relieved voice.

He shouted again.

'It won't be hard to take you,' he yelled. 'You ain't goin' no place without horses.'

Tom Riley fancied that he could hear some movement inside the house as one or more of the men tried to look out at the adjacent corral where their horses had been. He nursed the Spencer rifle in his arms and waited for some reaction from them.

A shot suddenly rang out and jets of red dust flew up from the ground in front of the marshal. It was a shotgun blast, harmless enough at the range but a sign that the men inside were losing their tempers at discovering that their horses were missing.

He levelled the Spencer and aimed at the building, patiently waiting for the first sight of a human being at door or window. The shooting had begun and his first shot would be a signal to the posse that they could open fire. They were all in position and the bank robbers were completely trapped.

'Your last chance!' he shouted.

There was another shotgun blast, not directed at the marshal this time, but at a clump of rocks where one of his men must have shown too much of himself. The marshal caught a slight movement at one of the windows and pulled the trigger. A volley of shots followed, tearing lumps of white adobe off the walls of the building as the whole posse opened fire with relish. The men inside began to shoot as well.

The two Indian guides sat beneath the shadow of one of the outbuildings. They were smoking peacefully, holding all the horses and watching events with placid contentment. It was not their fight and they made no attempt to join in. If white men wanted to kill each other, that was fine by them.

Mike Pearce came crawling along the ground towards the marshal.

'I think I got one of them, Tom,' he said excitedly. 'Over at the side window. I don't reckon on havin' killed him but he let out one almighty yell. They can't shoot for nothin', in there. How are you doin'?'

'We'll get them. They've no place to go and we've got all the angles covered. I gave them a fair chance to come out and they were fools not to take it.'

'I heard you shoutin', but I'm right glad they want a fight. I ain't forgot how damned foolish I felt back in that cell.'

The marshal managed a smile.

'Yeah, I'm feelin' pretty bad about that myself. If we get that money and gold back to the bank, you and me will be off the hook. They'll think we're a pair of heroes instead of a couple of stupid stable bums.'

There was a rifle barrel being pushed around the edge of the doorway and the marshal broke off to take careful aim. His gun kicked and a figure seemed to leap across the opening of the building and collapsed in a twitching heap.

'That's two of them,' Mike Pearce

said, with quiet satisfaction. 'Only one to go, Tom.'

The firing from the house ceased and a haze of acrid smoke was clearing from the scene. The members of the posse held their own fire and quietly waited for something more to happen. Birds could be heard singing in the sudden hush.

'Are you comin' out?' the marshal shouted.

There was no answer.

'Are they all dead?' Mike asked, in a suddenly nervous voice.

'Could be. I hit one. You got another. Maybe someone else got lucky as well. We'll wait for a few minutes and then I'll go in and check.'

'I'll cover you.'

'Then you'd better use my Spencer. It's more accurate than that thing you've got.'

Ten minutes passed in absolute silence and then the marshal decided that he had better do his duty. He doubled up and ran speedily towards the house, his pistol drawn, his eyes alert for movement. He ran at an acute angle so that anyone shooting at him from a window would be exposed to Mike Pearce's fire. To his relief, he reached the adobe building unscathed and knelt below one of the window apertures. He could smell the bacon and coffee and could see the dead body sprawled in the doorway.

He had hit the man squarely in the upper chest and the bullet had gone straight through. He recognized his victim, it was the dark, Mexican-looking fellow who had locked him in the cell. It didn't seem important now and the marshal raised his head slowly above the window ledge and peered carefully inside the one-roomed building. He could see another man lying on his face below a rear window. His head had been blown away.

Tom Riley was sweating. He tried to swallow but his throat was too dry. It had been like this so many times during the war. He looked back at the rocks and could see Mike Pearce with the Spencer ready at his shoulder. There was a sudden odd noise from inside the house and he ducked below the level of the window again.

It was a moan and a few muttered words of pleading.

He straightened up and went quickly around to the doorway. Stepping carefully over the body, he entered the building and found the third member of the gang. He was a youngster, not more than eighteen or so, crouched in the far corner, with both bloody hands clutching his neck. His face was chalky white and scared. He looked at the marshal and mouthed a few silent words. Blood was flowing from a wound in the side of the neck.

The marshal went back to the doorway and called in the rest of the posse. One of them was an old-timer who had considerable experience of gunshot and arrow injuries. The old man started to staunch the blood while Tom Riley and the others looked round the interior of the ruined building.

The gang's saddle-bags were heaped together in one corner and Mike Pearce started emptying them in a search for the bank's money and Salty's gold.

'I've got it, Tom!' he shouted excitedly, and the others clustered round to see what he had discovered. A cascade of banknotes fell out of the bag followed by paper packets of coins. The marshal made a hurried count and decided that they had recovered all the missing money. He waited anxiously while his deputy searched the other bags. There was the bank manager's gold watch and chain, a couple of silver watches, a gold brooch with a broken clasp, and a small pistol that the marshal examined carefully.

It was a Remington .41 calibre double-barrelled gun and fully loaded.

'That ain't no cowpoke's weapon,' one of the posse said derisively.

'No,' the marshal agreed. 'I imagine they took it from someone in the bank. Probably the manager. Is there no sign of the sack of gold?'

'There's a white sack over here,' Mike said, as he looked around the earthen floor.

He picked it up and handed the empty thing to the marshal. The bank's name was stencilled on it; there was little doubt that it was the bag that had contained Salty's gold.

'Then where the hell's the gold?' the marshal asked angrily.

'They ain't been no place to spend it, that's for sure,' one man said dubiously.

'They could have hidden it along the trail,' Mike suggested,

'Ask the kid.'

Tom Riley went over to the corner where the old-timer had managed to staunch the bleeding and had fashioned a pad and bandage out of some shirting that he was fastening round the lad's neck.

'How is he?' the marshal asked.

'Passed out,' the old man answered laconically. 'Lost too much blood, I reckon, and scared as hell.'

'Can we get him back to Willard?' the marshal asked.

The old man wiped his bloodied hands on the remains of the shirt he had been using.

'Doubt it,' he said. 'He's pretty weak and the least move will start the bleedin' again. It's best just to leave him here, Marshal. He ain't likely to last the night.'

'Hell! Well, let's eat and then get these other two under the ground. If he wakes up, give me a call because I need to talk to him urgent.'

The posse settled down to eat the bacon and drink the coffee that the robbers had been preparing for themselves. They sat around on the dirt floor congratulating themselves on the fight they'd been in. Everybody was rehearsing his story for the time they reached Willard and were bathed in the admiration of their fellow townsfolk. They were also thinking of a possible reward from a grateful bank to add to the posse fee.

The only two not really enjoying their triumph were the marshal and his deputy. Mike Pearce, for all his bluster, had never actually killed a man before, and was now faced with the probability that the young lad would shortly die. Marshal Riley had other worries. The most important part of their mission had eluded him: the gold dust was still missing. He sat despondently listening to the excited talk of the others.

After eating, the bodies were buried in shallow graves with the aid of a couple of rusting shovels that were found among the ruins of the farm. While the men were occupied in that task, the marshal crossed to where the young man lay. He was breathing with little bubbling sounds and blood was seeping from under the bandage and padding to trickle down across his shoulder. Tom Riley shook him gently.

'Fella, I need to talk with you,' he whispered urgently. 'Wake up, lad. I gotta speak to you.'

The young man stirred uneasily and

gradually opened his eyes.

'I feel awful ... ' he murmured, 'feel ... '

He focused his eyes on the marshal.

'Who are you?' he asked suspiciously.

'Marshal Riley of Willard. What's your name, son?'

'Manton. Jimmy Manton.'

'Well, Jimmy, you been one bad son of a bitch and I gotta take you in.'

'Yeah, I suppose. We robbed your bank. Yeah, it was good fun while it lasted. What about Pete and Eddy?'

'If they were your friends, they're as dead as mutton. You'll survive though. When we get you back to town, you can see a real doctor and he'll have you on your feet in no time.'

'Am I shot-up bad?'

'Bad enough, but you're young and you'll live to go to jail,' the marshal lied. 'You'll probably get a light sentence too, bein' only a kid. Tell me, Jimmy, what happened to the gold?'

'Gold?' the lad's voice was faint and he did not appear to be interested.

'Yes, the large sack of gold you got from the bank. Where is it?'

The lad managed a slight smile.

'It was the old drunk ... ' he whispered. 'He kept on about it ... on and on ... in the cantina ... '

'What old drunk?'

The young man stirred uneasily and more blood oozed from his bandages.

'It was at Moffat's cantina. We was sittin' there and we could hear him tellin' somebody about his gold ... he was well drunk.'

'So it was Salty who gave the game away,' the marshal mused. 'Couldn't keep his silly mouth shut.'

'Salty? Who's Salty?'

'Never mind, son. Just go on about the gold. Tell me where it is.'

'Well, he said as how he had all this gold in a bank. In Willard, it was. That was the name of the town. And he was keepin' it there until he'd gotten a thousand ounces. Pete decided to crack the place. It was an easy one and we got the lot. Pete's one clever *hombre*.'

'Yeah. He's bein' buried now.'

The lad ignored the interruption.

'It was there, just as he said. And all the cash as well. Even a few extra trinkets from the staff and from a customer. She was a fat old cow. Screeched her fool head off until I clipped her one. We should have got clean away . . . clean to Mexico . . . '

His voice faded and the marshal shook him roughly. He opened his eyes again.

'Don't pass out on me now, lad. What happened to the gold?'

The dying boy told him.

5

The boy died in the early hours of the morning, The posse buried him and set off for home at daybreak. They took the three extra horses with them, all content with the success of their expedition.

It took the best part of three days to get back to Willard and they were all glad to split up and go to their homes. The marshal stopped off at the jailhouse to wash and have a meal before calling on the mayor and the bank manager. He was in the middle of drinking his second cup of coffee when both men arrived to get the news. He told them what had happened and produced the money that had been recovered.

'What about Salty's gold?' Mr Wynn asked anxiously,

Marshal Riley held up the empty sack.

'Vanished,' he said dryly. 'But I got the watches and the brooch.'

He displayed the items on the desk, and picked up the Remington derringer.

'And the pistol,' he added. 'That'll be your gun, Mr Wynn?'

The banker nodded distractedly and took it.

'But the gold,' he pleaded. 'There's over ten thousand dollars' worth . . . '

The marshal shook his head. 'I doubt if it'll ever turn up,' he said. 'Could be buried anywhere along the trail and we'll never know where to look.'

The mayor nodded his agreement. He was a little wisp of a man with thick eyeglasses and a pale, wrinkled face.

'I think you've done well, Marshal,' he said warmly. 'Three bandits dead and none of our people injured. That'll teach gunslingers not to come into Willard.'

'But the gold . . . ' the bank manager whined.

'Write it off to experience,' the mayor snapped. 'You shouldn't have had so much of it around.'

'The robbers knew it was here,' the marshal explained. 'They heard Salty boastin' about it in a cantina. The old fool was drunk and told everybody within hearin' where he kept all the gold he panned from the creek.'

'Head office are going to be very annoyed,' Mr Wynn said tetchily.

'Talkin' of head office,' the marshal put in with deliberate cruelty, 'the posse seem to think that there might be a reward from the bank for the work they did.'

The manager's face took on an expression of deepest displeasure but he said nothing to aggravate the situation. Instead, he put the watch and chain back in his waistcoat and stuffed the derringer in a side pocket.

'I'll give these other watches back to my clerks in the morning,' he said huffily, 'and I'll take the brooch round to Mrs Morgan right now. Her husband bought it for her and she sets great store by it.'

He hurried out, a disappointed man who had not even said thanks for what had been returned to him. The marshal poured out a cup of coffee for the mayor and the two men sat on either side of the desk to savour their drinks.

Tom Riley told him of their adventures and of how the three robbers had died. He left out details of the conversation he had exchanged with the injured boy. They discussed the selling of the horses and saddles to pay the posse fees and, when that was done, the mayor raised the matter of the slaying of the man called Edward Forbes.

'If you could come up with his killer as well, Marshal,' he said, 'that would make the town a whole heap happier.'

'It would make me a whole heap happier too, Mister Mayor,' Tom Riley admitted. 'You see, it seems to be a local killin'. I believe that someone in this town shot that drifter. It wasn't done by a stranger who just happened to be around at the time.'

The mayor frowned. 'How can you be so sure of that?' he asked.

'Well, now, there were no strangers in the saloon that night. Mike Pearce asked around and nobody could recall anybody who wasn't a local. Then there's the horse.'

'What horse?'

'There weren't none: that's the point. Nobody heard a horse gallopin' away from Willard, and no one could tell me which way the killer went. That's 'cos he didn't leave town.'

'Then you are suggesting that one of our own neighbours killed him?'

'Exactly. The only people who couldn't have done it were those who could prove where they were at the time. The folks in the saloon, for instance, and folks at home with their families.'

'I don't like that, Tom,' the mayor said, shaking his head sadly. 'To think that one of our own . . . and for little money.'

'Money might not have been the reason, but we'll just have to wait and see. I have a feelin' that we'll get to the truth of it one of these days. It's a funny thing, you know, two happenings so close together and Salty Parker figures in it both times.'

'But only as an innocent party, surely?'

'I guess so. He was certainly in the Golden Nugget saloon when Forbes was shot.'

The marshal slept like a log when he finally got to bed and made a point of turning out very late the next morning. Mike Pearce was already on duty, trying to placate an angry mortician about them not returning to town with three corpses for burial.

'No way was we travellin' for three days with dead bodies across the saddles,' Mike shouted angrily. 'They'd have stunk up the whole town.'

'They may have been bad men, Mr Pearce, but they needed Christian burial!'

The marshal nodded. 'That's probably it. Look, Mike, let's play it safe. Go down to the telegraph office and send a message of thanks to the commander of Fort Barrett. And while you're at it, ask for a description of the man.'

The deputy hurried off and Tom Riley sat down at his desk to look at the message again. He was puzzled. Gold dust kept popping up like the chorus of a song. And it wasn't making a lot of sense. He waited impatiently for Mike's return.

It took the best part of half an hour and the deputy's face was a study in puzzlement when he finally arrived with another sheet of paper.

'It weren't Salty,' he said, as he handed it over. 'It were some tall, stringy fella with a Texican accent. Says so on that message sheet.'

The marshal read it slowly. It was exactly as his deputy had said, with the added information that the man was riding a sorrel horse with a Mexican saddle.

'I think I'll have to look into this,' Tom Riley said quietly.

'What the hell for? This news is several days old and he could be anywhere by now. It's all of twenty miles to Gila Rock, and then you'd have to start trackin' him. Leave it be, Tom. We've done all that's needed.'

'I just got a feelin' about it . . . '

'Tom, look at it this way. Suppose he got the gold from old Salty? Maybe they did some tradin'. Take my advice: if you must chase this around, ride out to Salty's place first and have a word with him.'

'I think that's a good idea,' Tom Riley said decisively. 'Salty appears to be at the bottom of everything that's happenin' around here lately. You run the town for a few hours and I'll go pay the old devil a visit if he's at home.'

The marshal rode out of Willard shortly after and moved his horse at a leisurely pace through the increasing heat. When he came in sight of the creek, he rode slowly along its bank, noting the old mine workings and the heaps of spoil from the days when panning had produced easy pickings for the hundreds of hopefuls who had camped all around the scrub-strewn hillsides.

Salty's hut could be seen in the distance. It was a dirty, yellowed adobe structure with a flat roof, built against the rocky slope of the hillside. There was some fencing at one end to house the old mule. The animal was there, its head poking over the woodwork and its ears alert at the approach of the marshal. He halted a few yards away from the house and called out to the occupier.

There was no answer.

He called again and then dismounted. The mule raised its head eagerly as the marshal went toward the corral and tethered his horse to the fence. The mule hurried nearer and nuzzled his hand. Then it began chewing at his bridle. He realized that this was not a gesture of friendship, but that the animal was hungry. He looked at the water trough and saw that it was bone dry. Neither was there any fodder in the corral. What grass had grown there was chewed down to nothing.

He called Salty again and still got no answer. The shutters were closed and the rough door was firmly shut. He looked around the slope of the hill with its multi-coloured scree and wondered if the old man was hiding up there with his Sharps rifle cocked and ready for action.

'Salty!' he yelled to the rocks above the hut. 'It's me! Marshal Riley. Come on out, you old curmudgeon. I want to speak to you!'

Only a scampering lizard disturbed the silence.

He picked up an old wooden bucket and went down to the creek to fill it. The mule drank gratefully and also took the bundle of grass that he rapidly gathered for it. This done, the marshal went towards the building and did not fail to notice that a length of rope was lying on the ground, one end tied to a post and the loose end chewed through by rough teeth. Salty's dog had fought its way to freedom from starvation and taken off. Tom Riley pushed open the heavy door and the awful smell hit him like a solid wall. The blowflies rose in a cloud and he backed out again.

Salty Parker was dead.

6

It took him an hour to dig the grave and he sat outside the building for a while longer before plucking up the courage to enter and remove the body. He had opened both windows by removing the wooden shutters. There was no glass but the lack of wind meant that the strong smell lingered on.

The marshal pulled out the old man's body amid the tangled bed clothes and laid it on the ground where he could see what had caused his death. He had been shot in the back, high up near the left shoulder. The bullet had gone straight through and there had been a lot of bleeding. It was easy to see that Salty had been trying to wrap up the wound in various pieces of cloth. He had managed to stagger into the hut after putting his mule into the corral, and had laid himself on the bed fully dressed.

Tom Riley looked around for the mule's saddle and noticed for the first time that it lay just inside the door. He examined it carefully and traces of blood were easy to see. He went to have a closer look at the now contented mule. There were streaks of dried blood down one of its flanks. It looked as if Salty had been bushwhacked on the way home.

After the burying was done, the marshal went back into the house for a closer look around. Most of the flies had dispersed but the smell still lingered. Salty's guns were missing, presumably dropped where he was shot or taken by the attacker. There had been no money or gold dust on the body, only a little red bank book. His old brass pocket watch on its leather thong was also gone.

The hut was surprisingly neat for a rough old man. His few clothes were clean and laid out in a pine chest. His food store was lined with oil cloth and its various contents neatly bagged and labelled. All his dishes were washed and the earth floor had been recently swept. There were even three books on top of the chest. A Bible, Washington Irving's life of the first president, and a volume on metallurgy. All were well thumbed. There was a large bottle of ink and a store-bought pen close by.

No intruder had been there and it confirmed that it was somewhere on the trail that the old man had been attacked. The marshal searched through the chest and came up with fifty-five dollars in silver, a bullet mould, a tin box of gunpowder, and a small bar of lead for casting ammunition for the Navy Colt. There was also a bundle of yellowing papers. They were all deeds to mines and the marshal smiled grimly at their presence. He put them in his pocket along with the money, and went out to get the mule ready for the journey back to town. There was nothing worth removing from the hut and it would just be left to decay unless some passing drifter decided to make a home in it.

He set out with the old mule in tow and reached Willard a couple of hours later.

'So poor old Salty was finally bushwhacked,' Mike Pearce said when he heard of the findings.

'Yes, and I reckon that whoever was flashin' gold dust at Gila Rock, knows all about the shootin'. I'm goin' out to that cantina and see if I can get me a killer. Old Salty was a rogue but I don't figure he had to die like that.'

'Your man will be long gone by now. The news was stale when the army sent it to you.'

The marshal shook his head. 'I gotta make the effort, Mike. You take care of things here in town and I'll load Salty's mule up with campin' stuff and head out first thing in the mornin'.'

Word went quickly around Willard that the old prospector was dead and a telegraph message was sent out about the suspect who had last been spotted in Blackett's cantina trying to convert gold into cash. It was late in the evening by the time the marshal had got rid of all his visitors and was ready to turn in for the night. Just as he had decided to shut up the office, the door opened and Mr Edgeton entered with his usual self-important air.

Mr Edgeton was one of the only two lawyers in town. He was a stout man with a handsome, dark face and fringe of whisker that was carefully dyed jet black. His clothes were custom made and he wore a massive gold watch chain across his waistcoat.

'Ah, just caught you, Marshal,' he boomed. 'I have this very moment heard the sad news and hurried to fulfil my obligations.'

The marshal looked at him with mouth slightly open. It was a source of continual wonderment to him why lawyers never bothered to talk like regular folk.

'Obligations, Mr Edgeton?' he echoed.

'What obligations are you talking about?'

'My duty to the late Nathaniel Parker, of course. He was my client.'

'Oh.'

Tom Riley was not used to hearing the old man called by his real name. He waved the lawyer to a seat.

'Then you mean, Mr Edgeton,' he said, 'that you had some legal business with Salty?'

'Of course. I am the sole executor of his estate. Assuming of course, that he is now officially deceased.'

'Oh, he's deceased all right. I done buried him myself up at the creek.'

The lawyer took the offered seat and the marshal, giving up hopes of going to bed, sat down also.

'I suppose you are certain that it was my client who was buried?' Mr Edgeton asked with a severely judicial expression on his handsome face.

'Well, he was wearin' Salty's clothes, lyin' on his bed, and altogether lookin' like Salty usually looked. You can always dig him up again if you don't wanna take my word for it.'

'I was just making sure, Marshal. Now, his estate . . . '

'His what?'

'Estate. All of which he possessed. His . . . er . . . shack, money, etc, etc.'

'Oh, I see. Well, I brought back his mule, its saddle, fifty-five dollars in cash, some gunpowder, a lead bar, and a bundle of mine deeds. The rest of the stuff was pretty worthless. Just rough old furniture, a few tools, cutlery, foodstuffs, and some clothes. He didn't own the shack. Just squatted there. His dog's missin'. It seems to have chewed its way through the rope when it got hungry enough. I reckon it'll join all the other coyotes up in the hills. It was half-wild anyway.'

'I see. Then I'll take charge of the items you did bring into town.'

'Not so fast there, lawyer man. You asked me for proof that Salty was dead; now I gotta ask you for proof that you're his executor.'

The lawyer's face darkened for a moment and then relaxed again as he realized that the marshal was not to be intimidated or overawed so easily.

'Quite right, Marshal,' he said graciously. 'You must of course have proof.'

He took a folded paper from an inner pocket.

'This is his will. You will see that at the top of the first page, I am named as sole executor. And here at the bottom of the last page, is Mr Parker's signature and the names of the witnesses. All correctly drawn up in my office.'

He showed the marshal the relevant passages and Tom Riley unlocked the desk drawer and took out the items that he had brought from the shack. The lawyer leapt on the money and the deeds, but simply brushed aside the gunpowder and bullet mould. His eyes lit up as he scanned the papers and he was too busy to notice the grin on the marshal's face.

'So Nathaniel owned six gold mines,' Mr Edgeton exclaimed, with a degree of reverence. 'My client was indeed a man of substance. Just as he told me.'

'Didn't you believe him?'

'Well . . . when a scruffy-looking old man comes to make a will and is talking in terms of several thousand dollars, it is rather difficult to give credence to his stories. I know he has an account at the bank, and he did maintain that he had a large quantity of gold lodged there. I didn't believe that story until the bank was robbed recently and rumours of several hundred ounces of gold started to fly around.'

'Oh, he was a good customer of the bank,' the marshal said quietly. 'I got his depositin' book.'

He took the little red book out of his pocket and handed it to the lawyer. He had already examined it very carefully and it had given up its secrets. The visitor's eyes widened greedily as he saw the entries of gold deposited every week.

'Jumping Je — !'

Mr Edgeton almost forgot his dignity for a moment.

'Mr Parker was indeed a very wealthy man,' he said. 'This gold must be worth ten or eleven thousand dollars. And he has a cash deposit as well. His mining was obviously extremely successful. And these deeds — '

'Are worthless, Mr Edgeton.'

'My dear fellow . . . '

'That's why he was called Salty. Salting gold mines was how he used to make his living in the old days. He never mined for gold when he could help it, Mr Edgeton. He just flim-flammed greedy people who thought they were dealin' with a silly old man. He'd move in on an abandoned claim, take over the registration, and wait patiently until some new prospector came along with more money than sense. Then he'd let them look over his claim after loadin' a shotgun with a little gold dust and blastin' it into the rock. The smart incomer would spot the signs of real gold and make him an offer. Salty would play hard to get but eventually sell at a reasonable price. Then he'd be on his way before the other fella found out who'd really been doin' the cheatin'. It was the oldest trick in the trade, and I reckon it made him quite a bit of money.'

'But that was years ago, you say. This gold dust that he paid into the bank every week, where did that come from?'

The marshal smiled enigmatically. 'I got my own ideas about that,' he said. 'But I can't speak about nothin' I can't prove.'

'Yes, yes. Quite so. But in law . . . ' — the man was choosing his words carefully — 'in law it is Nathaniel's bank account and is apparently his legally held estate. You are not disputing the legal position, are you, Marshal?'

'Oh, no. I ain't disputin' nothin'. You and the bank manager go ahead and sort things out between you.'

Mr Edgeton left shortly afterwards, secure in the knowledge that he had done his duty and that a fat fee would be his as executor of the dead man's estate. The marshal went to bed at last and slept soundly.

He set off in the morning for Gila Rock. It was the best part of two days' journey and he took Salty's mule with him to carry enough food and bedding for a week. The weather broke in one of those sudden storms that come and go in Arizona without doing much good for the pasture or cooling down the atmosphere. He was drenched and miserable for a few hours before the sun again dried everything off and shone as ferociously as ever. A few more miles of travel and the landscape looked as parched as though no rain had fallen for years instead of hours.

Gila Rock was just north of the river that bore the same name. It was a reddish-coloured butte that stuck up in a small flat plain that had once been a gold-mining area. A dozen or so huts of board or adobe still stood beneath the shadow of the rock and there was enough grazing for a few farms in the neighbourhood. It was also a staging post, and for that reason only, the cantina had survived, supplying a change of horses and a resting place for travellers.

Tom Riley reached it early in the evening when the light was just fading and some of the heat going with it. A slight breeze had risen as he tethered his animals outside the cantina and brushed the dust off his clothes. Three other horses were tied there, and half a dozen heavier animals were in the corral around the side of the building.

Blackett's cantina was a small place, crudely built of wood but with a wooden floor that made it a rather high-class establishment of its kind. There were oil lamps on the walls and Blackett himself was behind the small bar, a pistol in his belt and a shotgun on the ledge behind him. He was a big man, broad and muscular, with a cropped head and military-looking moustache. His eyes were a pale grey and as hard as flints. He looked at the newcomer with cool indifference but noted his Navy Colt and the shotgun under his arm. He also took special heed of the marshal's badge.

'Evenin',' he greeted his customer. 'Beer or whiskey?'

'Beer.'

Blackett put a glass tankard under the barrel and produced the drink.

'Come far?' he asked, as he put the money in the drawer.

'Willard.'

Blackett allowed himself to look surprised.

'You're a bit out of your territory then, Marshal,' he said quietly. 'I take it you're just passin' through.'

Tom Riley did not answer. He was looking around the room at the five or six customers who were sitting about watching him discreetly. None of them answered the description of the man he was looking for. He knew as well as anybody that he had no powers in Gila Rock, but he also knew how people like

Blackett needed to be handled if they would not co-operate with the law.

'I'm looking for somebody,' he said. 'A man who was here a few days ago tryin' to change some gold dust into cash money. Know who I mean?'

'Can't say I do.'

'That's a pity. The army remember him bein' here, and I kinda thought that a man in your delicate position might be only too willin' to help the law.'

Blackett stared at him for a moment as if he had to work out the meaning of the words.

'Delicate position?' he echoed.

'Yeah. You bein' an agent for the stage-coach line an' all. Stage lines are very strict about law and order, them carryin' so much valuable cargo and havin' passengers' safety to worry about. Makes them kinda jumpy at times. They like to think that everybody who works for them is right behind law enforcement.'

Blackett got the message and looked

around the room to make sure that none of his regulars could hear the conversation.

'Four days back, it was. Maybe five,' he said in a low voice. 'A tall fella, thin as a broom pole, and speakin' with a Texan accent He had a little bag of gold dust and wanted to change it. I couldn't do anything because I don't carry that sort of cash, and I don't have no scales to weigh it. So, when I turned him down, he offered me a watch. An old brass thing it was, but it were workin'.'

'Did you buy it?'

'No. He'd polished it up and tried to say that it was gold. I threw him out.'

'Any idea where he went?'

The man shrugged. 'Well . . . he was headin' north-east up towards the Salt River. I reckon he'll be tryin' each staging post along the route. He was a mean customer. and I watched him until he was out of sight. I didn't fancy havin' him turn back and try anythin'.'

'How was he armed?'

'A Remington in a holster, an old

Colt Navy in his belt, and he carried a Sharps rifle. One of the older models. What's he done, Marshal?'

Tom Riley hesitated for a moment. 'Do you know Salty Parker?' he asked.

The cantina owner's face relaxed a little.

'Sure. Known Salty for years. He calls in here every few weeks, gets drunk and tells everybody about his gold in the Willard bank. We all have a good laugh, but he's real serious.' His face darkened again. 'Nohing's happened to Salty . . . ?'

'I'm afraid so. He was bushwhacked and a little bag of gold dust, a Colt, a Sharps rifle, and his brass watch were taken.'

Blackett banged his heavy fist down on the counter.

'Well, damn me for a cross-eyed pole-cat!' he bawled. 'I knew I'd seen that goddamn watch before. That was your man, all right, Marshal. If you catch up on that bastard and get him into court, you can rely on me to swear him clean on to the end of a rope.'

'I'm glad to hear that, Mr Blackett. Thanks for all your help.'

'Where you aimin' to stay tonight?'

'Campin' on the trail.'

'Not tonight, man. You stay here. No charge. It's the least I can do for Salty.'

The marshal had a good bed that night. His animals were well cared for and he had a large breakfast before taking off in the direction that Blackett had indicated. The next coaching stage was a full day's ride, and having a mule in tow, he could not travel as fast as usual.

Miller's farm was a pleasanter-looking place than Gila Rock, but the result was still the same. They remembered the man, and another traveller had bought the brass watch for a dollar. The killer had not been able to change the gold and had moved on in the general direction of Fort McDowell.

It was on the fifth day that Tom Riley had his first piece of luck. He had taken his horse and mule down to the river for water and was consulting the rough map that he had of the area. He was near the junction of the Gila and Santa Cruz rivers and it was always possible that his quarry might move south towards Fort Barrett. The man would not know that all the lawmen had been alerted and that the army were also on the look-out for him. The marshal made himself a small fire and began to brew some coffee. It was while he was waiting for this to boil that he sensed something odd. He could not place it for a moment and looked at the river bank in bewilderment. The mule and the horse were standing up to their fetlocks in the water, quiet and sleepy. His coffee was beginning to smell good . . .

That was it!

He could smell wood smoke. And not from his own little fire. It was the odd smell of a damped-down fire. Wet and smouldering wood, so familiar to country folk who threw the dregs of the coffee pot on to the flames when they were breaking camp. There had to be somebody close by, somebody who had probably spent the night by the river and was now moving on.

The marshal gathered in his two animals and carefully tethered them to a bush for safety. He took his shotgun and quietly moved along the soft sand of the bank in the direction of the smell. His spurs sounded abnormally loud in the stillness and he bent down to remove them and slip them into his belt. They still made a slight noise and he left them on the sand to collect later. He walked warily, conscious of the fact that his own presence might already be known to the other person. He cocked the shotgun and sniffed the air. It might have been an overwrought imagination but he felt that he could also detect some cooking smells.

It was some ten minutes later that he came to a halt and crouched behind some bushes that overlooked a patch of level grass. He could see a few wisps of blue smoke rising from the clearing but could hear nothing that suggested the presence of a human being. Tom Riley peered carefully around the bushes to get a better look.

There was a fire just as he had suspected. Quite a big one but now partially doused and smouldering on the margin of the grass and river sand. There were hoof prints on the edge of the water, and some fresh horse droppings. He waited patiently for a while, keeping low and hardly moving. If there was a horse in the vicinity it would make its presence known sooner or later, even if the rider was trying to keep quiet and stage an ambush. The minutes ticked away and the marshal watched silently.

There was no sign of life.

He finally stepped into the open, shotgun at the ready, and his body alert for the slightest movement. Whoever had been there had departed an hour or more since. He had spent the night by the river, which accounted for the large fire and the well-chewed grass on which his horse had been feeding. Some grass had been crushed where a bed roll had lain and there was a little patch of bacon fat that had come from a frying pan. If this was his quarry, then the marshal was catching up fast, and that didn't make sense.

Tom Riley frowned. He should still be several days behind. Unless this was somebody else. He looked aimlessly around as if for inspiration — and found it.

The hoof prints told him why he was catching up with his man: the killer's horse had cast a shoe and he was slowing up.

7

Tom Riley went back to his own camp site and began hitching up his mule and horse. His coffee had nearly boiled away but he drank what was left of it and started off on his travels again. His crude map told him that the nearest blacksmith was at the next staging post. There was a cantina there at Cuchala Pass with a thriving farming community to justify a few stores, the smithy, and a livery stable. There was even a telegraph office where he could communicate with Fort Barrett and Fort McDowell. Cuchala Pass could be reached in about three hours, and if his quarry was not there, he would at least be able to alert other law officers then rest up for the night before deciding on his next move.

It was dusk when he arrived at the little settlement. It was a drab enough place, set in the mouth of the pass, with a plentiful supply of water from a nearby creek. Towering cliffs cut off the hot sunlight during the day and kept the buildings cooler than most other localities, and any wind there was, funnelled through the pass to add more cooling to the atmosphere.

The cantina was more northern than southern in its construction, It was a two storied building of horizontal clapboards, totally devoid of Mexican influence. The windows were clean and the place appeared to be well lit against the dying of the daylight.

There was no local lawman and Tom Riley knew all too well that he would be on his own against a man armed with two pistols and a better rifle than the shotgun he carried. When Blackett had told him that the man was in possession of a Sharps rifle, he had no doubt that it was Salty's gun. The old man had been proud of it and boasted of its accuracy at a distance. It was an early model but deadly in the hands of anyone who knew how to use it.

The marshal rode along to the livery stable where a large corral housed the exchange horses for the stagecoach. He was looking for a sorrel as had been described in the army telegraph message, There was none there and he rode back between the straggling buildings and eventually found the blacksmith's forge. The man was still working there, straightening an old plough share on a large anvil. He was a big, broad-shouldered man and the light of the forge was all the illumination he seemed to need for his work. The hammering stopped as the marshal approached.

The blacksmith looked up from his task as Tom Riley reined in his mount. He put down the hammer and wiped the sweat from his face. His pale eyes had already noticed the lawman's badge as the light of the forge caught and reflected on the metal.

'And what can I do for you?' the man asked in a hoarse, whiskey voice.

'I'm lookin' for a man who might have ridden in here on a sorrel horse that had a shoe missing. He was using a Mexican saddle and carried two pistols in his belt.'

The smith came into the open air and stood looking up at the lawman.

'Ain't you a bit out of your territory, Marshal?' he asked. 'Our nearest sheriff is over at Fort McDowell.'

'Yeah. I'm several days away from my town, but that don't alter the fact that I'm lookln' for somebody.'

'And what's he supposed to have done?'

'There's no *supposed* about it. If he fits the description I've given you, he shot an old man in the back and robbed him.'

'That ain't nice.'

The smith began to wipe his hands on his apron as he made up his mind.

'A sorrel, you say?'

'Yes, and he'd also be carryin' a Sharps rifle.'

Even in the dusk, the marshal could see that he was on the right track. The man's face was giving him away. Tom Riley placed one hand delicately on the butt of his gun. He had found in the past that it had quite a profound effect upon the memory of reluctant witnesses. He leaned over his pommel.

'Where's his horse?' he asked bleakly.

The blacksmith looked for a moment as though he were going to argue, but the pistol and the shotgun made up his mind for him.

'Round the back,' he said reluctantly. 'I've already put on a new shoe and he's pickin' it up in the mornin'.'

'I doubt it. So where is he now?'

The man hesitated but his eyes strayed inexorably in the direction of the cantina.

'Thanks,' the marshal said dryly.

He spurred his horse across what passed for a street and dismounted outside the wooden-frame structure. There were only two other horses tethered there. Tom Riley removed his badge and stuffed it into his waistcoat pocket, mounted to the boarded sidewalk and stepped into the lighted building.

The bar was a small one, most of the place being taken up by lodging-rooms. A short, immensely stout man with sleeked-down black hair was behind the counter. His olive face was as smooth as that of a baby but the eyes were dark and wary. They were the eyes of a man who missed nothing, and were full of calculation. He watched the lawman approach and delivered him a professional smile.

'What'll it be?' he asked.

'Beer.'

Tom Riley looked around the room. There were only three people there and none of them fitted the description of the man he was chasing. He paid for the beer and drank it quietly. It tasted better than he expected. It was always possible that his quarry had taken a room and was having an evening meal somewhere.

'Where can I get something to eat around here?' he asked the bartender.

The man smiled. 'Right here. There's a dining-room just through that door and it's the best food for twenty miles. I eat it myself.'

He patted his stomach to prove the point.

'Thanks. I'll give it a try.'

The marshal walked slowly towards the doorway to the right of the bar. He pushed aside the heavy curtain and entered the small room that contained two tables covered in yellow oilcloth and a central oil lamp that hung from the ceiling. The place was clean and smelled of freshly cooked food. Two men sat at one of the tables, and both looked up at the entry of the third diner.

One of the men was small, a thin-featured fellow in his middle forties who wore city clothes and looked totally out of place in a southern cantina. The other was tall and painfully thin, with a seamed face and predatory eyes. He fitted the description that the marshal had received. The small man seemed rather relieved at the entry of somebody new and he gave Tom Riley a welcoming smile. His fellow diner just looked up from his plate and then went on eating.

A stout woman who looked part Indian served up a mess of meat and potatoes with some thick gravy. The marshal tried it and found the taste to his liking. He dug into the food hungrily and helped himself liberally to the newly baked bread.

'Come far?' the little man asked.

'Fort McDowell,' Tom Riley replied. 'I'm on my way to take up a job with the McEwen ranch. They're hirin' for a cattle drive up north.'

'That sounds exciting sort of work. I'm in boots and shoes. Representing Miller and Dawson of Tucson.'

'Tucson? That's one big city, I guess,' the marshal said, in feigned admiration.

'And very modern, let me tell you, sir,' the little man said proudly. 'We've just about got everything these days. And so many folks you wouldn't scarcely believe. All packed into one grand city.'

The meal went on amid casual conversation. The third man made no attempt to join in. He just ate stolidly and, when finished, rose from the table and headed for the door. Tom Riley saw what he expected to see. The man had a Colt revolver and a Remington at his waist. The Remington was in an old army holster but the Colt was just thrust through the leather belt.

The marshal rose quietly, pulled out his own Colt and came up behind the man. He thrust the cocked gun into the small of his back.

'Just keep your hands well above your waist, friend,' he said firmly. 'Otherwise, I'll be blowin' your spine to pieces and spoilin' your digestion.'

The man stopped in his tracks and slowly turned his head. He raised his hands as ordered.

'If you're holdin' me up, fella,' he

said harshly, 'I ain't got nothin' worth stealin'.'

'I'm takin' you in for murder,' Tom Riley told him. 'I'm the Marshal of Willard and you're wanted back there for the killin' of Nathaniel Parker.'

'I don't know no Nathaniel Parker.'

'Maybe you didn't exchange names when you shot him in the back. You're wearin' his Colt and you sold his brass watch for a dollar. When I get around to searchin' your belongings, I reckon to find his Sharps rifle too. Satisfied?'

'I never been to Willard . . . '

'Look out, Marshal!'

The cry was from the little salesman and Tom Riley swung round to see what was happening behind his back. The fat woman was coming at him with a large butcher knife raised in her right hand. Her face was a mask of fury as she lunged at him. He managed to swing away and struck out wildly with the Colt, catching her across the side of the head with the barrel. She let out a yelp and dropped the knife.

The gunman drew the Remington from its holster and cocked it as he swung round on the marshal. He was too late. The lawman's gun was already cocked and it went off with a devastating noise in the small room.

The bullet tore into the killer's right forearm and he dropped the heavy pistol as he let out a yell of agony. The gun went off as it hit the floor and a chunk of plaster flew off the opposite wall. He grabbed furiously for the Colt at his belt and had it halfway out when the marshal fired again. He did not miss his target this time. The bullet entered the man's chest and he slumped against the curtained doorway and then collapsed in a heap on the boards.

Tom Riley now had time to deal with the woman but his blow with the barrel of the gun had put her out of action. She was huddled in a corner holding her bleeding head and moaning softly.

The fat bartender came rushing in with a sawn-off shotgun thrust out before him. He found himself looking down the barrel of the marshal's Colt and decided that heroism was a little out of place.

'Before you get any silly ideas,' Tom Riley said calmly, 'I'm a marshal and this man is wanted for murder. So just put that gun down and we'll not fall out. A big fat man like you would take a lot of killin'. I might have to put three or four bullets in your gut to make sure you got the message.'

The bartender smiled his oily smile and placed the shotgun on the dining-room table.

'It's not my fight,' he said unctuously. 'He just stays here now and then. Maria is his woman.'

'And what is she to you?'

'She's my sister. She don't mean no harm, Marshal, but she took up with this no-good and he always comes back here when things get too hot for him. He's a no-hoper, believe me.'

Tom Riley smiled a little.

'That's true enough at the moment,'

he said. 'He'll be dead in the next minute or two.'

He leaned over the fallen man and began searching his pockets. He found Salty's bag of gold and the marshal took it along with the Navy Colt.

'I'm also lookin' for a Sharps rifle,' he told the bartender. 'Where is it?'

'It'll be in their room. Up the stairs at the back there and the second door on the left.'

Tom Riley turned to the little shoe and boot salesman who was still sitting at the table, fascinated by the whole noisy affair.

'Thanks for your help,' he said. 'I'm much obliged. What's your name?'

'Devlin. Philip Artemis Devlin,' the man replied eagerly. 'You're certainly very welcome, Marshal. This is the first time I've ever seen a gunfight. Most exciting.'

'Only for the winner, Mr Devlin. The other fella ain't so lucky. Thanks, all the same.'

The lawman took the bartender's

gun and removed the percussion caps from the nipples. He then went upstairs and, in a stuffy little bedroom, he found Salty's rifle. When he came down again, the woman had disappeared and the bartender was behind the bar as though nothing had happened. The body still lay in the doorway of the dining-room.

'I hope you're goin' to remove that,' Riley said as he was leaving. 'It'll start smellin' in the next week or so.'

The bartender managed a weak smile at the joke and watched with hostile eyes as the lawman left the building.

★   ★   ★

Tom Riley rode back to Willard in a reasonably contented mood, He had dealt successfully with the bank hold-up and with the murder of Salty Parker. They had been cleared up in pretty fast time, and if being imprisoned in his own jail still rankled, he could console himself that those who had humiliated him were dead and buried. He was the town hero. There was only the death of the prospector that nagged him slightly. It was obvious that he had been slain for the fifty dollars that Salty had given him, but something in the whole set-up was puzzling. The marshal chewed on it like a hound on a bone all the way to town. He gradually came to the conclusion that he knew who had killed Edward Forbes, and why.

8

As Tom Riley had anticipated, he was the hero of the hour when he returned to Willard. He called on the mayor to make his report, and his success was discussed by the town council. Some of the members were even enthusiastic enough to propose a rise in his wages. That particular rashness was quickly knocked on the head by more experienced councillors who reminded their colleagues that it was not their job to squander public money that could best be spent on themselves.

He paid a call on Salty Parker's lawyer that same day in order to hand over the gold and the two firearms. This was a very cordial visit and Mr Edgeton was only too happy to receive the dust but was less enamoured of the guns, which timidly he put away in a cupboard in his comfortable office.

'There is a little matter I'd like to bring up,' the marshal said to the lawyer after he had received thanks for his work. 'It's about the makin' of Salty's will.'

'Yes? What about it?' The man's voice had an edge of suspicion.

'I was kinda wonderin' when he did it.'

Mr Edgeton hesitated for a moment and then went to a large filing cabinet. He took out a folder and laid it on the desk in front of him.

'I'm not sure that the question is relevant, Marshal,' he said primly. 'But I assume you have a good reason for asking.'

'Well, there are still one or two points to clear up, and I was wonderin' if some particular event caused Salty to make a will, or if it was somethin' he'd done years ago.'

'I see. Yes, that's good thinking.'

Mr Edgeton opened the folder and took out the document.

'The precise date was the eighth of

July this year,' he said. 'That at least was the day he came to see me. I had the will ready for his signature the following week. Does that help you?'

The marshal crossed to the large calendar on the wall of the office.

'Then I reckon,' he said, as he slowly worked out the dates, 'that he came to see you the morning after that man, Edward Forbes, was shot.'

The lawyer looked a little puzzled.

'Yes, I suppose that would be the case. Is it important?' he asked.

'I'm just gettin' the times right. You see, Salty was worried when Forbes got himself killed. He stayed in town that night and I took him home the next morning. So the only time he had to see you, would be almost as soon as your office opened for business the next morning.'

The lawyer nodded eagerly.

'You're absolutely right. He was on the doorstep that day. I hadn't thought about it before, but that was the way of it. He certainly appeared to be somewhat agitated, told me that he hadn't much time, because you were picking him up shortly. He gave me all the information I would need to draw up the will and said that he'd be in the next week to sign it. We members of the legal profession do not like being rushed, but he was very anxious, and I felt obliged to comply with his wishes. Does it have significance?'

The marshal pulled a face. 'I don't know,' he admitted, 'but it seems to have been the murder of Forbes and not the bank hold-up that persuaded him to make a will. He'd had a bit of money for all those years and never bothered. Then all of a sudden, he's thinkin' about dyin'. I was wonderin' why, that's all.'

'Old age does funny things to a man, Marshal.'

'Yeah, but if Salty was scared of gettin' killed, it wasn't by the man who actually did it. That gunslinger was just a passin'-through sort of fella. He spotted Salty tryin' to change gold dust in the saloon and followed him along the trail. He wasn't the man Salty was afeared of.'

'And you seriously believe he was afraid of somebody?'

'Yes. The man who shot Forbes.'

The lawyer sat brooding on it for a moment or two.

'I recall the mayor saying that you believed he was killed by someone living here in Willard,' he said after a while. 'Is that true, Marshal?'

'Yes, sir, That's true. Forbes seems to have been the only stranger in town that night.'

'And . . . may I ask . . . have you any idea who it might be?'

'I ain't positively certain, but I got me a few pretty good ideas on the matter. Nothin' for a court of law, you understand. Tell me, Mr Edgeton, who gets all Salty's money?'

'Ah, yes, of course. He has a granddaughter who lives in Santa Fe. She's a school ma'am, so he told me. I've sent a letter to her and am awaiting her instructions.'

'Sounds a bit complicated, workin' at that distance.'

The lawyer allowed himself a superior smile.

'We're used to that sort of thing, Marshal. I shall sell off Nathaniel's bits and pieces, arrange money drafts to be sent to her, and organize everything with the co-operation of the bank. In cases like this, a little touch of sympathy, and a smooth transfer of funds, is what is required.'

'Is she married?'

'No, I gather that she's a maiden lady who, until recently, lived with a widowed mother. Miss Parker is the only daughter of the late William Parker; he was Nathaniel's son by a second marriage. I believe that his first wife was of Indian extraction.'

'She was a Chiricahua,' the marshal said dryly.

'Quite. Nathaniel told me that he had two sons by that . . . er . . . liaison. They have apparently joined their own people and do not benefit from his will.'

'I wonder if they know he's dead,' the marshal said softly.

It had not occurred to him before that Salty's sons were somewhere out there, unaware of their father's murder.

'I doubt if they know,' the lawyer said dryly. 'How would one contact people like that? A smoke signal or a formal call?'

'Smoke signals might be safer. I hear tell they're ridin' with Cochise, and they'd love a scalp like your'n.'

The two men exchanged mirthless laughs and the marshal took his leave after shaking hands. He went out to the street, breathing in the dry hot air and idly noting what was going on around him. There was a familiar figure descending from a gig and tethering the horse to the rail outside the dry goods store. The marshal could not place the man for a moment and then realized that it was the little boot and shoe drummer who had saved him from the knife attack in Cuchala.

Tom Riley crossed the street at a leisurely pace and looked at the contents of the gig. There were a couple of large wooden cases, a carpet bag, and a number of painted wooden boards advertising boots and shoes. He grinned and went about his business.

★   ★   ★

The stagecoach arrived a week later. It was one of the few days in the year when rain fell on Willard. A sudden storm erupted early in the morning, drenched the whole town for a few hours, and then vanished like snowballs in Hades. The main street resembled a quagmire when the stage pulled in with its passengers, its collection of mail and luggage, and the strongbox for the bank.

The marshal did not even bother to leave his office. The roof had leaked and he was only just getting through mopping up the mess. Mike Pearce had been called to the livery stable where three horses had broken loose in panic at the thunder and lightning and were now being rounded up somewhere outside town.

He was a little surprised when somebody knocked at the door and waited without entering as most folk did. Tom Riley dropped the mop and went across to open it.

A pretty girl stood there. Not just ordinary pretty, but also elegant in a citified way. She wore a pale-grey dress and bonnet to match. Her figure looked good and her dark hair was set in a large bun that was held in a lacy-patterned snood. There was a gold-edged jet brooch at her collar and she carried a large carpetbag that looked heavy.

The marshal stared at her in surprise. He was conscious of the broad, smiling mouth and arched, delicate eyebrows above deep violet eyes.

'Well . . . er . . . come on in, ma'am,' he finally managed to say.

He took the carpetbag from her and

offered the most comfortable chair. She sat down carefully, keeping her skirt from touching the damp floor.

'We've had a bit of a flood,' he explained quickly. 'It's still a little wet.'

'We passed through the storm on the way here,' she said. 'It was frightening for a while.'

'Would you like a cup of coffee, ma'am?'

'Thank you, I'd love one. You are Marshal Riley, aren't you?'

'Yes, ma'am. What can I do to help you?'

She took the proffered cup in both hands and sipped the liquid eagerly.

'That's better,' she said with a smile. 'My grandfather said I should look you up. I'm Louise Parker.'

9

Marshal Riley's encounter with Miss Parker was the best thing that he could remember happening to him in all the years he had been a lawman in Willard. He commiserated with her on the death of her grandfather and gave her all but the more gruesome details of what had happened to the old man. She listened without expression, squeezing the coffee cup in her hands as though to keep them warm, and taking a refill when he offered one.

'You've come a long way,' he said, when the story was told. 'I believe Mr Edgeton thought that everything would be dealt with in the mails.'

She smiled a little sadly. 'My grandfather wrote to me a few weeks ago,' she said. 'He didn't correspond much, and the letter came right out of the blue. He said in it that there'd been a recent killing in Willard and it made him realize he was getting old. He wrote me that he had made a will and that there was a lot of money in the local bank. He didn't trust banks or lawyers so he told me to come here and look after things myself. He also said that the only man in town to be trusted was Marshal Riley.'

'That was kind of him. I had a soft spot for old Salty. I also happen to think that he gave you some good advice.'

She looked at him quizzically.

'Don't you trust banks and lawyers either?' she asked.

'Not particularly. What are you going to do now then?'

'Well, after booking into the hotel, I'll call on the lawyer and let him know I'm in town. Then I'd like to see where grandpa lived and is buried.'

Tom Riley jumped at the chance.

'I'll take you out there,' he said quickly. 'We'll get a gig from the livery stable and pack a few eatables. Come back here as soon as you're free.'

Gallantly he escorted her to the hotel and then walked back to his office in a strangely happy mood. He noticed that the boot and shoe salesman was back in town, driving the same large gig and delivering wooden crates to the dry goods store. The little man staggered under the weight of his merchandise and the marshal went across the street to have a word with him. He waited until he came out, brushing down his city suit and rather red in the face.

'Mornin' to you, Mr Devlin,' the marshal greeted him.

The man looked taken aback for the moment as if not recognizing the lawman.

'Land sakes!' he exclaimed, extending his hand. 'I'd not thought to see you again, Marshal. How are you keeping?'

'Fair enough. How's business?'

The little man's face lit up. 'Better than I thought,' he said cheerfully. 'I was here last week and picked up a good order from Mr Hanks. Just delivered it now.'

'You're lucky. He's reckoned to be one hard-nosed Yankee.'

The man laughed. 'Then he knows a bargain when he sees one.'

The drummer nodded in the direction of the hotel.

'Would that young lady you were escorting just now . . . would that be Mrs Riley?' he asked.

'No. As a matter of fact, she's the granddaughter of the murdered man. Miss Parker.'

'Ah, how sad for her. Then all that business is settled then?'

'I guess so. She's here to wind up his affairs and then she'll be off again to Santa Fe.'

'Santa Fe? That's a real long journey, Marshal. I hope it was worth her while.'

The man was getting too nosy and Tom Riley did not respond to the implied question.

'She must think so,' he said in a neutral voice.

They exchanged a few more casual words and then the little man climbed to his seat on the gig, gave the marshal another handshake, and took off down the street.

Tom Riley watched him go with a frown on his face. For a timid city mouse who seemed out of place in a rough part of the territory, Mr Devlin was carrying a very handy-looking pistol hidden inside his fancy coat. The marshal hesitated and then went into the store. Will Hanks was already opening the two wooden crates with the help of his sour-faced wife.

'Mornin', Marshal. Come to see our new ridin' boots?' the storekeeper asked. 'They're better than all the old army cast-offs that have been hangin' around for the past few years.'

The marshal picked up one of the boots he was shown and weighed it in his hand.

'They look all right,' he said absently. 'Tell me, Will, what do you know about this Devlin fella?'

The storekeeper stopped his unpacking.

'Know about him?' he echoed. 'I don' know nothin' about him 'cept that's he's a push-over for a price. Poorest drummer I ever did see.'

'Does that mean you got this lot cheap?'

Will Hanks grinned. 'Sure as hell does, but don't spread it around. That man ain't got the sense he was born with, and it's no business of mine to put him right. You . . . er . . . worried about him, Marshal?'

'Maybe. This company he sells for, you ever heard of them before he came on the scene?'

'Can't say as I have. Tucson is a place I never got around to visitin'. You ain't tellin' me he's sellin' stolen goods, I hope?'

The marshal shook his head. 'No, I don't think so,' he said. 'Maybe he's just new to the game. If I were you, I'd buy all he's got while the goin's good.'

'And that's exactly what I aim to do. He's acomin' back with more next week, and I'll have the cash money waitin' for him.'

The marshal went back to his office thoughtfully. He stood at the window, staring into the street, watching the steam rising from the wet sand as it dried out under the bright sunlight. Miss Parker came out of the hotel, hesitated a moment, and then walked along the boards until she had to cross to the lawyer's office. She lifted her skirt delicately and manoeuvred her path through the mud. Tom Riley smiled at her easy way of tackling the problems of a small town without paved streets and drainage. He wondered what sort of town Santa Fe was.

She came out of Mr Edgeton's office after a while and stood for a moment, looking up and down the street. Then she lifted her skirt again and crossed over to the bank. Tom Riley decided it was time he went along to the livery stable to borrow the gig and call in at Ma Preston's for some of her cooked chicken and pie, all neatly packed away in a hamper. Ma Preston could be relied on for a good outdoor meal, nicely presented and not too dear.

It was an hour later that Miss Parker called at the marshal's office. The gig was outside, ready to go, and Tom Riley had shaved specially for the occasion. He left a slightly bemused Mike Pearce in charge of things and helped the young lady on to the gig. Then he climbed up himself, placed his shotgun in the rear, and set off for Salty's old home.

They talked of various things during the drive. Nothing very personal, but all with a comfortable feeling that can exist between two people who just get on together. The marshal pointed out the places of interest and, as they reached the creek, he described the gold rush and the mine workings that had once been so thriving. She made intelligent rejoinders but gradually became more silent as they got nearer to Salty's hut.

When they reined in there, she sat for a while, gazing at the scene, and staring at the mound in the reddish ground that was now her grandfather's grave. The marshal was glad that he had taken trouble over it. He had buried the old man neatly and covered the mound with a layer of flattish sandstone rocks that gave it some proper semblance of a hallowed spot.

'I'm glad he's buried here,' she said softly. 'It was his home and he was probably happiest here.'

The marshal helped her down, feeling the warmth of her small hand in his large sweaty one. She pulled off her bonnet and went over to the grave.

'I couldn't take him back to town anyway,' he explained rather reluctantly. 'He'd been dead for a few days.'

'I understand. You did the best thing. Didn't he have a dog?'

'Yes. A really vicious brute. It took off into the hills. Don't worry, it'll survive.'

'Did he have a horse?'

'No, an old mule. I got here in time to save it from starving, and handed it over to lawyer Edgeton. He'll have sold it by now, along with Salty's guns and saddle. As executor, I reckon he turns everything into cash and hands it over to you.'

She nodded.

'Yes, that's what he said. It's always sad to see a man's things sold off. I saw it happen when Pa died, and then I had to do it myself when Ma passed away.'

The marshal looked around, and his eyes narrowed a little. He went back to the gig and lifted out his shotgun. The girl's eyes were questioning.

'Something wrong?' she asked a little fearfully.

'I doubt it, but someone's been here very recently.'

'How can you tell?'

He pointed to the ground.

'Two lots of visitors, I'd say. Some Indian ponies a few days ago before the storm. They're unshod. Then there's a bigger horse belonging to a white man. That was after the rain.'

'You can tell all that?'

'Easy enough. The white man went into the hut but the Indians didn't. I think they came here to pay their respects to Salty.'

'What did the white man come for?'

The marshal grimaced. 'Who knows?'

He bent over the grave and began lifting the stones one by one. At the fourth attempt, he found what he was looking for. Some small beads and feathers that had been laid reverently out of sight.

'Were they put there by Indians to honour my grandpa?' Louise asked in a small voice.

'I reckon so. Your grandpappy was a friend of the Apache. He respected them and they respected him. Did you know about his first wife?'

'My father told me that he lived with an Indian woman. Is that what you mean?'

'Yes. As far as he was concerned, he was married to her. They had two sons. I don't think they're around to do this, but some passin' braves left these tokens of respect on their behalf.'

Tears started at the corners of her

eyes and she made no attempt to wipe them away.

'I think that's rather nice,' she said softly. 'And I have two Indian uncles. The folks back home would never believe this. It's too much like something out of Washington Irving.'

The marshal snapped his fingers.

'Washington Irving,' he repeated. 'Salty had a book written by him. It's in the hut.'

'So he kept it. I sent it to him when it was first published. He once said in a letter to Pa that he admired George Washington. So I sent him Irving's life of the president. Is it there now?'

'I guess so. I left it on the chest with his Bible and another book. Let's go see.'

He led the way into the hut. The door was slightly open and the place had obviously been disturbed. The three books lay on the table and the chest had been opened. Some of its contents had spilled on to the earth floor and it was clear that somebody had been searching.

'Our white man did this,' the marshal said grimly. 'He ain't got no respect for the dead.'

Louise Parker picked up the Washington Irving book. It was dusty but otherwise undamaged, She held it to her breast and looked around the building in awe.

'How could he live like this?' she asked.

'Oh, this was neat enough when Salty was alive. He had everything he needed and he kept the place clean. Just look at his clothes. They're worn enough but they've all been washed. He folded them neatly away in that chest and did all his chores, regular like.'

The girl picked up the large copper dish that was used for panning gold.

'Is this what he used?' she asked.

'Well, it's what he would have used if he'd been pannin'. Did Mr Edgeton tell you about Salty's gold?'

'Yes, he said that there was a lot of it

and that it had been stolen from the bank. They're sending cash to replace it and we have to wait until it arrives. I would have settled for a bank draft but they tell me that grandpa ordered the cash money just before he died. It should come in on the next stage.'

'I see. Did your grandpappy ever tell you where he got his gold?'

She shook her head.

'No,' she said. 'I suppose I took it for granted that he mined or panned for it. Didn't he?'

'Well, if he did, it wasn't any place known to the locals. All the gold was mined out years ago. You see, Miss Louise, there was a belief that Salty was a bit of a villain . . . '

She laughed a little and displayed her small even teeth. 'Oh, I knew that,' she said. 'Pa used to tell me stories about him. I do know how he got the name of Salty, if that's what's worrying you. But he did do some honest mining now and then.'

'Oh, granted. But not five ounces a

week, every week, for two years. I don't want to disappoint you, but it may be that Salty got this gold dishonest like. If that's the case, you could lose the best part of your inheritance.'

'I see. And what's your opinion?'

'Well, I'm a marshal and I gotta uphold law and order. Of course, if nobody makes a complaint, and I don't know anything official, then there ain't a lot I can do.'

The girl thought about it for a moment.

'Mr Edgeton tells me that with the sale of all Grandpa's belongings, and with what's in his bank account, my inheritance will be about six hundred dollars. By the time I pay his bill and allow for my fare to Willard, I'll still have over five hundred. By my reckoning, that's a heap of money, Mr Riley. It's a lot of dollars in one big lump for a schoolteacher. When I was told there was another ten thousand coming in on the stagecoach, that seemed like a fairy-tale. So that's how I'll treat it. If it was stolen or got in any other dishonest way, then it can go back to the rightful owners. I'll be content with what I know is mine.'

Tom Riley grinned. 'Well, maybe it won't happen,' he said. 'Maybe it will all come to you, with nobody claimin' they was robbed.'

She looked around the room again.

'Let's go into the open,' she said quietly.

They emerged into the bright sunlight and breathed the air deeply. The marshal took the hamper from the gig and carried it to a clear spot near the creek. Quickly he gathered some kindling and lit a little fire for the coffee pot. They sat side by side, eating and drinking in perfect harmony and a few birds came down to feed on the crumbs.

'It's peaceful here,' the girl said after a while.

'Yes. It's a bit hard to imagine that there were once several hundred miners up and down this creek, with tents right along these banks, and all those holes in the hillside lit with candles while they dug out the veins. They left it in one awful mess, but things are smoothin' over now. The weather sees to that. When are you headin' back home?'

Miss Louise shook her head. 'I don't know. Everything depends on how fast Mr Edgeton moves. It'll be two weeks at least, I suppose. I'm not looking forward to another journey like that.'

'Are the trains so bad?'

She laughed.

'We've got no railroad in Santa Fe. It's getting nearer, but I had to travel by stage, then train, and then another stage to get to Willard. It wasn't easy, Marshal.'

'I guess not. Maybe you could stay here in Willard. That is, if you ain't got no kin back home.'

'Why should I stay here?' Her glance was challenging.

'Well . . . we have a school . . . ' Tom Riley stumbled on, 'And I do know that the mayor is on the look-out for a new school ma'am to replace Mrs Boyle. She's nigh crippled with the rheumatics and wants to retire. It's quite a good school. Two rooms and near to twenty kids. There's a room above for lodgin', and the pay ain't bad.'

The marshal ground to a halt. He had said too much and blushed furiously. A thing he hadn't done since being locked in his own cell.

'It was just a thought,' he ended lamely.

'A rather interesting one,' she said, with an easy smile. 'Let's wait and see, shall we?'

They started back for home soon afterwards, driving slowly and enjoying the late afternoon sun. They sat in greater intimacy than on the outward journey.

Tom Riley was enjoying the long day in the company of this pretty woman, and only one thing was spoiling it for him.

He knew that they were being followed.

10

Marshal Riley dropped his passenger at her hotel and drove the gig to the livery stable where a lad took care of it and began unharnessing the horse. He then went back to the main street and strolled in a casual way towards his office, carrying the empty basket and his shotgun. He went inside, closed the door behind him and took up station at the window.

Mike Pearce was sitting at the desk whittling a piece of wood. He looked up in astonishment.

'What's up, Tom?' he asked.

'I just want to see if anyone comes ridin' into town in the next few minutes. Somebody has been followin' us all afternoon.'

'Well, I'll be . . . Don't he know no better than to trail a lawman? He could have got dead.'

'He might yet,' Tom Riley grunted. 'And here he comes now.'

Mike Pearce joined him at the window and both men watched as the boot and shoe salesman rode slowly along the main street on a large raw-boned horse and went round the corner towards the livery stable.

'That little runt was followin' you?' the deputy asked in astonishment.

'He certainly was. Indians had been around Salty's place a day or two ago. Just payin' their respects. But there were other footprints. Narrow ridin' boots like the ones he sold Will Hanks. Fancy town stuff that ain't been seen around here in an age. They were fresh made tracks after the rain. I reckon he was sniffin' around and then crossed our trail as he was on his way back to town. So he followed us all afternoon.'

Mike Pearce gave a lewd grin.

'Well, I sure hope as how you didn't embarrass the man,' he chuckled.

'No, I didn't. Though I came mighty close to embarrassin' me.'

They both laughed.

'Well, Tom, what are you goin' to do about this peeper?' the deputy eventually asked.

'Nothing yet, I want to be sure what game he's playing. Why the hell is Salty at the bottom of everything that happens round here?'

The conversation more or less ended on that note and the marshal turned to other matters such as some missing cattle on Morrisey's farm. He didn't take it too seriously. Old man Morrisey lost cattle the way other people lost hair. His sons were too idle to herd the animals properly and then the marshal was plagued with lurid stories of rustling.

Tom Riley went to bed early that night. He slept soundly and opened the office after a good breakfast and a fresh shave in case he encountered Louise Parker again, He intended to make a point of seeing her if it was at all possible. There had been a few women in the life of the marshal but this one seemed to be something special.

Mike Pearce came in a few minutes later. He was grinning broadly and pointed towards the street as he entered the building.

'Somethin' hoppin' down at the bank,' he said. 'It ain't opened and all the old women are panickin' in case their money's not safe. I reckon Pennington Wynn overslept.'

The marshal did not see it as something funny. He went to the door and looked down the length of the street. A few people stood outside the closed doors of the bank and the younger of the two clerks was speaking to them, as if trying to reassure everybody that nothing was wrong. There was no sign of the other clerk or of the manager.

'I think I'd better go down there,' the marshal said softly. 'Keep an eye on things here, Mike. I'll fire a shot in the air if I need you.'

He buckled on his belt and took the shotgun under one arm. Mike Pearce accompanied him to the door and stood watching his boss as the marshal walked swiftly but with dignity towards the town's monument to fiscal prosperity. The younger bank clerk, who was distinctly on the wrong side of fifty, looked rather relieved to see him. A few ladies gathered round the two men and a couple of store owners now joined the little group.

'What's happenin' here?' the marshal asked.

'Mr Wynn must have overslept,' the clerk explained. 'Eddy's gone down to his house to rouse him out. I've told them that it's only a matter of minutes and we'll have the place open for business.'

A few minutes passed and the crowd grew larger. Marshal Riley began to worry, and his agitation was not eased when he caught sight of the other clerk coming round a corner, sweating in his high collar and dark coat, and obviously distressed about something. The man held a bunch of keys in his right hand

and hurried to the bank door to open it.

'Where's Mr Wynn?' the other clerk asked anxiously.

Eddy looked at the marshal and at his colleague. Sweat was dripping from his bony nose.

'Let's get inside first,' he muttered, and turned the key.

Tom Riley followed the two men into the bank and a mass of people crowded after them. Most of them had no reason to be there at all, but human nature being what it is, they were all anxious to be in on somebody else's problems. The older clerk led the marshal straight through to the manager's office while the other teller stayed at the counter and tried to sort out the genuine customers from the merely inquisitive.

When the door of the manager's office was tightly closed behind them, Eddy sat down on a chair. His hand was trembling and he looked thoroughly upset. The marshal, knowing where Pennington Wynn kept his good whiskey, poured out a tot for the distraught man, and not wishing him to drink alone, poured one for himself.

'All right,' he said, after they had both taken a good pull on the liquor, 'tell me what it's all about.'

'Marshal, I can't believe it . . . there must be a mistake . . . '

The man was clearly distressed.

'Take it easy, fella. Just start at the beginning.'

The clerk took another sip of the whiskey and started on his tale.

'We arrived at the usual time this morning, and Mr Wynn didn't turn up. It's most unlike him. He's usually here on the dot. We waited for a while and then one or two customers began to arrive. I thought it best to go round to his house and see what the trouble was. Mrs Wynn was alone. She said that he'd taken off about eleven o'clock last night for Fort Barrett on urgent bank business. He'd rented a horse earlier in the day from the livery stable, and packed a few things for the journey. He must have known about it before we closed yesterday, but never told us. I just can't understand . . . '

'Are those his keys?'

'No, that's what took me so long. When Mrs Wynn told me that he'd gone and taken the keys with him, I had to go home for my own spare set.'

'Will they open the safe?'

'Of course.'

'Then I think you'd better open it.'

The man swallowed some more of the whiskey and rose from his chair.

'Marshal, you're not suggesting . . . ' he began.

'Just open it, Eddy.'

The clerk's trembling hand swivelled the cover on the brass lock and inserted the key. It turned easily and he swung open the heavy door. The safe was empty of money.

'I think you need another drink,' the marshal said helpfully.

'I think I do. Surely we must be wrong, Marshal. Mr Wynn can't be a thief.'

'I'm afraid he is. He's gone off with every cent in the bank, and he's had all night to get away from here.'

'Mrs Wynn mentioned Fort Barrett . . . '

'Not within a hundred miles of it. He'll have ridden to the rail depot at Siller's Bluff if he's any sense and caught the early train due west. Any idea how much was in the safe?'

'I can tell you exactly as soon as I get out the ledgers.'

The bank clerk took three heavy volumes from the safe and began working out details of the various balances. He put down his pen with a sigh.

'To be precise, Marshal, the figure is seventeen thousand, one hundred and eleven dollars and thirty cents.'

Tom Riley resisted a temptation to grin.

'He might have at least left us the thirty cents,' he said gravely.

'It's a disaster. What am I going to do?'

'Well, just go out there and tell them that the bank's closed until further notice; head office will take care of everything and all their money is safe. You may as well let them know that Wynn has gone off with the cash. They're bound to find out soon enough anyway. Then come back here and answer a few questions for me.'

The man hesitated.

'Go on, man,' the marshal urged him. 'If you handle the thing right, you could be manager this time next week. Just be firm with 'em.'

The clerk departed reluctantly and Tom Riley sat himself in the manager's large leather chair. He looked around for a cigar but Mr Wynn appeared to be a non-smoker. The marshal took another drop of whiskey instead.

It was fully ten minutes and after a lot of shouting that the clerk returned to the manager's office and sat down opposite the lawman. He picked up his glass and finished off what was left of the whiskey.

'They're not very pleased,' he said shakily. 'They almost attacked me out there. I've closed up and sent Bill home. There's no point in us being here, is there?'

'None at all, and when you've answered one or two questions, you might as well go home yourself. Don't forget to telegraph the news to head office and I'll inform all the law officers and the army. He's had a long start on us so I'm not very hopeful.'

He offered the man another drink and it was not refused.

'Now,' the marshal began, 'I want to hear about Salty's gold.'

The man looked completely puzzled.

'I don't know anything,' he said. 'Besides, it all went in the hold-up. You know that. It's cash money he has in the bank now, waiting to be picked up by Mr Edgeton and given to Miss Parker.'

'How much cash was sent by head office for Salty to collect?'

The clerk looked at one of the ledgers.

'Ten thousand, two hundred and forty dollars. That was the value of the gold, less the bank's commission. Then he had an account with another four hundred and fifteen dollars.'

'So that was included in the money that Mr Wynn took?'

'Yes. Head office sent us Salty's cash because that was how the old man wanted it, and they also replaced the rest of the cash that was taken in the hold-up. That's why we had so much at one time. I still can't believe that Mr. Wynn . . . '

'Eddy, did you ever see Salty's gold?'

The man looked startled. 'Well, of course I did. I took five ounces off him every week for two years, measured it out and brought it to this office to be added to his store. Of course I saw it.'

'Did Mr Wynn put it in the bag in front of you?'

'Of course . . . ' The clerk stopped and thought about it. 'Well, not exactly. I left it on this desk and he got the big white bag out of the safe.'

'And then he filled the bag with some sand out of that spittoon, Eddy. Salty came round again by the back door, collected his five ounces of gold, and brought it along to you again next week.'

'My God! You mean that they were partners?'

The marshal nodded. 'Yes, and I'll wager that the original deposit was made in this office, and you never saw that either. Just a white bag stored in the safe and entered in the ledgers as Salty's gold.'

'Jumping Jiminy!'

'The way I work it out, Eddy, is that they planned to have the bank held up when there was enough sand in that bag. Salty was always a rogue and there was no way he could get that much gold dust around Willard Creek. He and Wynn were building things up for a big bust. Salty travelled round the territory, drinkin' at every low cantina. He'd boast about the gold he had stored in this bank, and sooner or later, some smart gunslingers was goin' to raid that little nest egg. Then Wynn would claim the cash value of the gold from head office and he and Salty would have an easy few thousand apiece.'

The clerk thought it over.

'And then Salty got killed,' he mused.

'Exactly. And left all his money to his granddaughter. Poor old Wynn wasn't even goin' to get a half share. It was all in Salty's name and he couldn't fool lawyer Edgeton. So your manager either had to give up the idea, or do what he did and steal everything. He seems to have told Miss Parker that the money hadn't yet arrived. When did it actually get here?'

'Same stage she came on. In a strong-box under the driver's seat like always.'

'So that's why he chose last night.'

The clerk looked curiously at the marshal. 'And you worked all this out?' he asked.

Tom Riley tried to look modest.

'Bit by bit,' he admitted. 'Do you remember the afternoon of the day when that prospector was shot dead behind the livery stables?'

'That Forbes man? Yes, I suppose so.'

'Well, Salty rode into town that mornin' and came to the bank as usual.'

'I remember.'

'How much cash did he withdraw?'

'Same as always. Ten dollars.'

'Did he come back to the bank later in the day?'

Eddy thought ahout it for a moment.

'That's right. He did. Said he wanted to see Mr Wynn and I brought him in here. He was quite a time with him.'

'Did he make another withdrawal?'

'No. Just spoke to Mr Wynn.'

The marshal nodded contentedly. 'That's what I thought,' he said. 'He came here to tell Wynn that some stranger was pesterin' him for a stake. I reckon that stranger must have guessed somethin' about the gold. Or if he didn't, Wynn and Salty thought he did.

So Wynn gave Salty the fifty dollars to grub-stake him, and when Salty had handed over the money, Wynn was waitin' behind the livery stable with that derringer of his.'

'He shot Forbes?'

'I'd take a heavy bet on it. Then he took back his fifty dollars, and that scared the hell outa Salty. He began to realize how ruthless his partner was. So he made a will.'

'But how do you know Mr Wynn gave him the fifty dollars?'

'Because Salty never carried much on him. Too risky when you travel alone. He didn't have the money when he met the stranger, so he had to get it from somewhere. And I don't think he drew it from his account. I saw his depositin' book, and there was no fifty-dollar withdrawal.'

The marshal stood up and patted the elderly clerk on the shoulder.

'Don't let it worry you too much,' he said kindly. 'Mr Wynn fooled everybody. Just wait till all his respectable friends hear about this. He'll be the talk of the gospel hall.'

He went back to his office to write out the telegraph messages and found Mike Pearce already in receipt of an incoming one.

'The telegraph clerk sent it along, Tom,' the deputy said excitedly. 'Is it true that bank manager Wynn's skipped town?'

'Yes, and with all the money. He's a hundred miles away by now.'

He took the proffered telegraph form and read it.

'I don't get it,' Mike Pearce said. 'We don't know any Pinkerton man.'

'I think we do,' the marshal said with a grin. 'He sells boots and shoes and calls himself Devlin.'

11

According to the telegraph message, Mr Devlin was lying wounded at Siller's Bluff. Willard was the nearest town with a marshal and the telegraph clerk had automatically informed Tom Riley. There was little other information except to say that the Pinkerton detective had been in a shoot-out with a wanted man. And the wanted man was Pennington Wynn, the respected bank manager now on the run with $17,000 dollars.

'Well, at least it accounts for him following me and working as a shoe drummer,' the marshal said cheerfully. 'The bank must have employed him to check on Salty's gold. I wasn't the only suspicious one, so it would seem.'

'Are you goin' out there, Tom?'

'Sure am. It means that he caught up with Wynn, and I think I know how. He would have been informed by the bank's head office that the money was on the stage. So when Wynn told Miss Louise that the cash hadn't yet arrived, Devlin knew otherwise, and he must have guessed that the manager had no choice but to make a run for it. He probably didn't speak to Miss Louise, but I reckon he had a word with her lawyer. Little Mr Devlin isn't as simple as he looks.'

'So I stay here and you ride out to Siller's Bluff?'

'That's about it. Telegraph ahead for me and ask them to have a spare horse. I might have to trail Wynn and mine will be pretty tired when I get there.'

'Right, but won't Wynn have used the railroad from the Bluff?'

'It depends where he met up with Devlin. The shootin' might have stopped him boardin' the train and there isn't another one for three days. My guess is that he's on horseback. Same as me.'

'But a lotta hours ahead.'

'Yeah.'

The marshal was able to set off an hour later, travelling at a steady pace so as not to tire his mount too much on the five-hour journey to the rail depot. Siller's Bluff was a small township in the middle of a farming area, with a good water supply and some pasture that was sheltered by trees and had a better rainfall than other parts of the territory. The railroad found it a convenient halting place because it was central for several other townships, and the cattle trade was gradually developing as the marauding Indians were driven further south into Mexico. The water was also a determining factor; railway engines needed water in large quantities.

Tom Riley stopped only once for a short break and arrived at the spot just after four in the afternoon. He reckoned to have made good time and went straight to the telegraph office, which was a small wooden hut at the side of the rail tracks. It doubled as a ticket office and the clerk looked as if he was glad to see a new face in town.

'If it's Mr Devlin you're wanting, he's at the doctor's house, Marshal,' he said. 'Got himself shot in the leg. Best bit of excitement since Ma Smith's cat got tree'd by a hound dog.'

He pointed out the white-painted house of the medical man and the marshal rode down the long sloping street of the almost empty little place and tethered his horse at the picket fence.

The doctor was a large, untidy man, a cigar in his hand and ash covering his ample grey beard. He took the lawman into his front room where little Mr Devlin sat on a large fabric-covered chair with his right leg thrust out before him and a rug thrown across the lower part of his body. He looked quite well, still neatly dressed and wearing his city coat. An array of dinner dishes took up space on a small side table and he greeted the marshal with an amiable smile.

'I'm afraid my secret's out,' he said, as they shook hands. 'You must forgive me for not taking you into my confidence but I didn't know how things were in Willard. The bank was sure that fraud was going on but they couldn't pin it down. I suppose you guessed some of it yourself.'

The marshal nodded and explained how he had stumbled on the truth of the story.

'I reckoned there was no gold,' he said, 'and if Salty was pullin' some sort of flim-flam, he had to have a partner inside the bank. Who better than the manager? But why did you follow me?'

'Because you were with Miss Parker and she stands to gain.'

'Well, I reckon she's a sweet young lady who's goin' to be a little disappointed, but no more than that. She's inherited enough legal-like from her grandpa to keep her happy. So what happened between you and Wynn?'

The detective gave a resigned heave of his shoulders.

'Well, I knew the money had arrived in town, and with all that cash in the bank, and Miss Parker's lawyer due to withdraw a big chunk of it, Wynn had to make a run or lose everything. I hurried things along a bit by talking to his clerks in the saloon. They almost certainly went back to their boss and told him that there was a stranger in town asking questions about the bank's business. That helped make up his mind for him. If he ran for it, that proved my case.'

'Well, he certainly ran for it. And where were you at the time?'

The detective smiled ruefully.

'Outwitting myself,' he admitted. 'I was already here, waiting for him to arrive. He came in half an hour before the train was due and went up to get a ticket at the telegraph office. He had two carpetbags. They were on either side of his saddle when he got here, and you can be sure that the money was in one of them. All I had to do was to step forward, arrest him, and take the cash

169

back to the bank.'

'And?'

'Marshal, I must be getting too old, or too trusting. I never figured for him having a gun, but he saw me approach, pulled a derringer and opened fire. Got me in the calf of the leg and I just fell there on the street. Couldn't move a step. I pulled my gun but he was off like a streak of lightning. The town was roused so he couldn't go for the train. Folks tell me that he went back to his horse and lit out for places unknown.'

'His horse will be pretty tired then?'

'I reckon. Now, lying here, I've been thinking about the problem. He's about six hours ahead of you, and he can't use the railroad any more because the word is out for him. He'd be trapped on a train. He needs another horse, or some place to rest up where there is no telegraph. He can't get into Mexico on his present animal, so he'll head for the junction of the Colorado and Gila rivers. There's a township there at the quartzite workings. It's off the beaten track and there's no lawman or telegraph. He could change horses, rest up a while, and then cross the mountains into California or go south to Mexico. It's his best bet.'

The marshal thought about it for a while. He was envisaging the thirty or more miles he would have to ride.

'My horse won't do it,' he said, 'but I telegraphed ahead and the livery stable here should have one ready for me.'

'Use mine. It'll save money. It's rested up and I won't be riding for a week or so.'

The marshal had a meal, washed up at the local eating-house, and then rode out on the rather large animal that Mr Devlin had used, and which, though a roan gelding, was a spirited thing that seemed to have been overfed on corn. He got proper management of it after a while and headed almost due east at a steady pace.

He bedded down that night in the open air. If anything, it was even hotter than he was used to and he slept fitfully.

He was on the edge of desert country with mountains in the distance. The rocks were stratified with wondrous colours and when he threw a drop of water over some, they came alive like polished precious stones. It was mid-morning when he sighted the quartzite area and the little cluster of primitive huts that made up the community of miners.

There were some cattle around, feeding on poor grass, and there were several corrals of horses. Smoke came from a stone chimney at the end of one of the huts, and outside was a small board advertising meals of meat, bacon, and eggs. He dismounted wearily and hitched his horse to the post.

The interior of the eating-house was smelly and dark. There were just four small tables and a stove on which all the cooking appeared to be done. An elderly woman, her grey hair streaming down both sides of her face, was bending over a frying pan that was smoking more than the outside chimney. She looked up when the marshal entered, her glance predatory and sharp.

'You're the first,' she said. 'It's deer meat today. Cost you fifty cents.'

'I'm lookin' for a man. Well built, short fella, dressed up in city clothes. Speaks well. Seen him?'

She put down the frying pan and came closer to look at the lawman in the gloom. She took notice of the badge and her lip twisted in a sort of smile.

'I mighta seen him,' she said. 'But I'm too busy to take much heed of other folks doin's. You goin' to arrest him?'

'Yeah.'

She came closer and he could smell her sour body.

'What's he done?'

'Killed somebody and robbed a bank.'

She cackled. 'Well, ain't he a mighty man for a soft-speakin' dandy.'

'So you've seen him?'

173

'I didn't say that.'

'You didn't need to. Maybe you don't know it, lady, but when a bank gets robbed, there's a pretty good reward to the people who help recover the money.'

She considered his words carefully.

'I mighta seen him,' she said. 'Fancy-dressed bastard who turned up his nose at my good steaks. Said they weren't cooked enough. He had a couple of carpetbags with him and wanted to know where he could do a horse trade.'

'When was this?'

'Last night. Late customer he was.'

'And where did he go when he left here?'

'Well, we ain't got no livery stable so I sent him to Matt Coley. He buys and sells near everything.'

The marshal sighed. 'And where will I find Matt Coley?' he asked patiently.

'Are you certain sure there'll be a reward?'

Tom Riley gave the woman a

five-dollar bill and watched her stuff it into a pocket under her apron.

'That's just on account,' he said.

'Matt's place is just down by the big corral next to the smithy. You can't miss it.'

The marshal found the place easily. It was another dirty-looking hut that sold all sorts of ironwork and saddlery. Matt Coley was a large man who hadn't shaved for a few weeks and who was dressed in an old army singlet that looked as if it had not been near water since the war ended. He was an ugly man with a protruding lower lip and narrow forehead below cropped hair.

'Yeah, I sold a horse to the fella you want,' he said, without being pressured. 'Snooty sort of city gent he was. What's he done?'

'A killing, and a bank robbery.'

'Now, ain't that a wonderment? I never figured him to have the guts for that sort of thing. Well, he traded me his horse, bought himself another, and then lit out in the direction of the border.

Seemed pretty anxious to be gone. Didn't even haggle over the price.'

'Well, thanks.'

The man smiled broadly, exposing blackened teeth.

'Don't be in such a hurry, Marshal,' he said. 'I ain't told you everything yet. I figure myself for a businessman.'

'And you aim to make a profit?'

'Every time. Now, I'd bet that Ma Donovan didn't send you along to me out of the goodness of her sweet old heart.'

The marshal handed over another five dollars and watched it disappear in the man's pants pocket.

'So what else have you to tell me?' he asked.

The man gave a sly grin. 'He won't be goin' too far, Marshal. And he won't be movin' fast. I clean forgot to shoe the horse I sold him, and he's got to cross some mighty rough ground.'

The marshal looked hard at the man. 'Surely he'd notice?' he said.

'Marshal, he was a man in one

almighty hurry, and besides, he weren't no horseman.'

'Thanks, Mr Coley. You're a nice man to do business with.'

After a short rest and a meal from his own stores, the marshal rode on in the general direction of the Mexican border.

At dawn the next morning he was on a high bluff and was able to survey all the land to the south of him. The mountains were to his right and left with a moderately gentle valley between, scattered with a few trees and plentiful scrub. He sat his horse and watched the scene for any sign of life.

There was a cloud of dust some way down the valley. He screwed up his eyes to make it out better but dust was all he could see at that distance. Strangely enough, it seemed to be coming nearer rather than receding. Then he realized why: there was another haze of dust some distance behind the first. Somebody was being chased along the floor of the wide valley.

As the clouds drew nearer, he could see a lone horseman being pursued by three other men. They were gaining slightly on him and the lone horseman was hampered by two large, colourful carpetbags that swung on either side of his saddle. There was little doubt that the man being chased was Pennington Wynn, and the marshal could now make out the identity of the pursuers.

They were Indians, and he could hear faint snatches of their shouts coming to him on the wind.

Tom Riley spurred his horse down from the bluff to get to the valley floor before chased and chasers reached his position. He guessed that the desperate man would ride over the smoothest ground on his failing horse, and that was near an outcrop of rock behind which he led his own animal.

He dismounted and took the shotgun out of its holster. From his position, it was now more difficult to see any distance, but he waited patiently until the first rider came into view. The man was galloping towards him, and the marshal could see the sweating animal and its terrified rider quite clearly as they reached a point about fifty yards ahead of him. The Indians were still another hundred yards or more behind.

'Come right past me!' the marshal shouted.

The rider looked about him in terror for a moment, and then located the voice. He turned his horse slightly towards the jumble of rocks and passed the marshal with only a few yards to spare. Tom Riley caught a glimpse of a tense, pale face.

'Keep going!' he yelled.

The man merely nodded and galloped on.

The lawman crouched down behind the rocks and waited for the pursuing Indians to appear. The first of them was on a small white pony. He wore an old army hat and was waving a flintlock musket as he came within range. The marshal stood up and emptied one barrel of the shotgun at him. The charge took the man full in the left side and he tumbled to the ground while his pony galloped on.

The next Indian was only a few yards behind. He tried desperately to stop and the marshal fired the second barrel at almost point-blank range. Most of the charge hit the man in the face and he fell backwards from his horse.

The third rider was some way behind and he reined in hurriedly. He carried no gun but had a serviceable bow which he now began to make ready. The marshal drew his Colt and fired a single shot at him. The range was too great but the pony reared as if it was hit. The Indian loosed off an arrow and galloped away.

Marshal Riley watched him go, and then picked up the arrow, which had missed him by quite a few feet. It was a hunting arrow, not one flighted to penetrate the horizontal ribs of a human being. Wynn had just been unlucky enough to meet a party out for food, and they'd taken the opportunity to attack a lone white man.

He mounted his horse and went off after the fleeing bank manager. He knew it would not be difficult to catch up with him. The man's horse was almost on its last legs, and the rider was not in much better condition.

He was within shooting distance of the man some ten minutes later. The errant banker had slowed down, not through any wish of his own but because his mount was dropping with fatigue. He reined in at the sight of the lawman.

'I'm not a fighting man,' he shouted. 'I'll go along with you, Marshal, but just let's be civilized about this. After all, it's only money.'

'You killed Edward Forbes,' the marshal shouted back. 'And you wounded a Pinkerton detective man. That ain't exactly friendly. So just raise your hands in the air and keep them there until I say otherwise.'

The banker slowly did as he was told

and big patches of sweat showed under his arms.

'The money's all there, Marshal,' he said ingratiatingly. 'Every last cent of it. There's enough for two.'

The marshal rode closer with the Colt in his right hand. He was half expecting the banker to make a move and was not disappointed. The man kneed his horse very slightly and the animal automatically moved round to the right. Pennington Wynn put his hands down to the reins as though to check it, but one hand suddenly flew to an inner pocket and the derringer appeared.

Tom Riley fired and the banker tumbled from his mount. He lay on the ground, clutching his side where the bullet had entered. The marshal dismounted, collected the fallen derringer, and checked the carpetbags. The money was all there, just as the man had said. He bent over the injured banker and examined the wound.

'Am I badly hurt?' the man asked quietly.

'I reckon so. Can you get on your horse?'

'No, I feel too weak. It's not painful, but . . . ' He stared up at the sky. 'I'd rather die here than in some jailhouse. Just stay with me till it happens. That's all I ask.'

The marshal stayed with him and Pennington Wynn died about an hour later. Tom Riley managed to hoist the heavy body on to the tired horse and began the slow journey back to the quartzite mines. He had noticed a small burial ground there, and that was where the banker could rest for eternity.

★ ★ ★

It took nearly five days for Tom Riley to get home to Willard. He had telegraphed his success ahead and was welcomed like a conqueror when he arrived. The mayor, the council, and Mr Philip Artemis Devlin were all there.

Mr Devlin was leaning heavily on a stick but his little face was alert and smiling when he greeted the marshal and supervised the return of the money to the bank.

It was later in the jailhouse that Tom Riley was able to relax with Mike and the Pinkerton man.

'It all ended very well for you, Marshal,' Devlin said, as he took a small sip of whiskey. 'Better than a trial. Saves a lot of money and fuss, and stops some smart-ass lawyer man from hoodwinking a judge and jury.'

He raised his glass.

'So here's to Marshal Riley. A job well done.'

'And so say I,' the deputy chipped in.

The marshal tried to look modest. He took out his pocket watch and noted the time. There was someone he wished to visit.

'If you fellas will excuse me . . . ' he said casually. 'I have one or two chores.'

'Not at the hotel, by any chance?' Mr

Devlin asked in a suddenly serious voice.

'Eh . . . yes.'

'Miss Louise?'

'Yes. I want to tell her about the inheritance.'

'No need. She knows all about it and she left town.'

The marshal let out an audible sigh of disappointment.

'Gone? But I thought . . . '

Devlin put down his glass.

'Tom,' he said sorrowfully, 'I've got some bad news for you. Louise Parker got the money and lit out. She got all of it. All the value of Salty's gold.'

Tom Riley shook his head in bewilderment.

'But that's not possible. I brought every cent back. You were there to count it.'

'Tom, just remember that she came in on the same stage as the money. She'd been in touch with the head office, prepared to take a draft on her local bank. They told her that they'd sent the cash to Willard at her grandfather's request so that she must collect it there or wait a long time for another transfer across the country. She knew exactly when it was arriving. So you can see what she did?'

'No, I can't. I just seem to be a dim hick marshal with a straw in my mouth.'

'She went to the bank on the day she arrived, and when Pennington Wynn told her that the cash wasn't there, she called his bluff. I don't know how much she knew about her grandfather's activities, but she suggested to Wynn that he give her a draft for the cash payable at the Tucson branch. She told him to send a telegraph to confirm it. He was only too happy to oblige. So she got the draft, lit out of town in a hired gig, cashed the draft in Tucson before they got news of Pennington's flight, and then she vanished.'

Tom Riley sat for a moment in stunned and hurt surprise. Then he began to see the funny side of things

and started to laugh. Mike Pearce
joined in and only poor Mr Devlin
remained silently disapproving.

THE END

We do hope that you have enjoyed reading this large print book.

Did you know that all of our titles are available for purchase?

We publish a wide range of high quality large print books including:
Romances, Mysteries, Classics
General Fiction
Non Fiction and Westerns

Special interest titles available in large print are:
The Little Oxford Dictionary
Music Book, Song Book
Hymn Book, Service Book

Also available from us courtesy of Oxford University Press:
Young Readers' Dictionary
(large print edition)
Young Readers' Thesaurus
(large print edition)

For further information or a free brochure, please contact us at:
Ulverscroft Large Print Books Ltd.,
The Green, Bradgate Road, Anstey,
Leicester, LE7 7FU, England.
Tel: (00 44) **0116 236 4325**
Fax: (00 44) **0116 234 0205**

Other titles in the
Linford Western Library:

THE CHISELLER

Tex Larrigan

Soon the paddle-steamer would be on its long journey down the Missouri River to St Louis. Now, all Saul Rhymer had to do was to play the last master-stroke of the evening. He looked at the mounting pile of gold and dollar bills and again at the cards in his hand. Then, looking around the table, he produced the deed to the goldmine in Montana. 'Let's play poker!' But little did he know how that journey back to St Louis would change his life so drastically.

THE ARIZONA KID

Andrew McBride

When former hired gun Calvin Taylor took the job of sheriff of Oxford County, New Mexico, it was for one reason only — to catch, or kill, the notorious Arizona Kid, and pick up the fifteen hundred dollars reward the governor had secretly offered. Taylor found himself on the trail of the infamous gang known as the Regulators, hunting down a man who'd once been his friend. The pursuit became, in every sense, a journey of death.

BULLETS IN BUZZARDS CREEK

Bret Rey

The discovery of a dead saloon girl is only the beginning of Sheriff Jeff Gilpin's problems. Fortunately, his old friend 'Doc' Holliday arrives in Buzzards Creek just as Gilpin is faced by an outlaw gang. In a dramatic shoot-out the sheriff kills their leader and Holliday's reputation scares the hell out of the others. But it isn't long before the outlaws return, when they know Holliday is not around, and Gilpin is alone against six men . . .

THE YANKEE HANGMAN

Cole Rickard

Dan Tate was given a virtually impossible task: to save the murderer Jack Williams from the condemned cell. Williams, scum that he was, held a secret that was dear to the Confederate cause. But if saving Williams would test all Dan's ingenuity, then his further mission called for immense courage and daring. His life was truly on the line and if he didn't succeed, Horace Honeywell, the Yankee Hangman would have the last word!

MISSOURI PALACE

S. J. Rodgers

When ex-lawman Jim Williams accepts the post of security officer on the *Missouri Palace* river-boat, he finds himself embroiled in a power struggle between Captain J. D. Harris and Jake Farrell, the murderous boss of Willow Flats, who will stop at nothing to add the giant sidepaddler to his fleet. Williams knows that with no one to back him up in a straight fight with Farrell's hired killers, he must hit them first and hit them hard to get out alive.

THE CONRAD POSSE

Frank Scarman

The Conrad Posse, the famous group that had set about cleaning up a territory infested by human predators, was disbanding. The names of the infamous pistolmen hunted down by the Posse were now mostly a roll-call of the dead, but the name of the much sought Frank Jago was not among them. That proved to be a fatal mistake for it was not long before Jago took to his old trail of robbery and murder. Violence bred violence, and soon death stalked the land.